CELTIC FOLK-TALES FROM ARMORICA

"There is a twofold meaning..... a literal and a mystical, and the one is but the ground of the other."

John Smith the Platonist.

F.M.LUZEL

CELTIC FOLK-TALES FROM ARMORICA

Rendered into English, with an introduction and commentaries, by Dr. Derek Bryce

Published by Llanerch Enterprises, Llanerch,
Felinfach, Lampeter, Dyfed, Wales, SA48 8PJ.

ISBN 0947992049

Printed by Cambrian News, Aberystwyth.

CONTENTS.

Translator's Introduction.

Amongst the Celtic peoples, the Irish and Welsh have a written literature coming down from ancient times. The Bretons, on the other hand, have no ancient written documents, but they have kept an oral tradition, embodied in songs and stories, passed from one generation to the next. In modern times these songs and stories have been collected, written down, and often translated into French. Luzel's collection of stories was made in the 1860's and 1870's, before the time when storytelling had suffered from the influence of radio and television, but at a time when school education was already weakening the tradition. Despite this last comment, we must remember that some of Luzel's storytellers would have learnt from grandparents and others who were born back in the eighteenth century.

Many of these stories are of ancient, pre-Christian origin. They have suffered modification during the Christian era. It is understandable that such modification has occurred, for it was necessary that the stories remained understandable to their listeners, and that they did not contradict their established beliefs. Many of these stories, however, are esoteric in character, and in some cases they have been modified unintelligently from an exoteric, rather than esoteric, Christian point of view.

The problem with stories passing from the old polytheistic traditions, to the monotheistic Christian tradition, has been partly semantic. We speak of 'Gods' in the old traditions, and 'God' as the supreme being in Christian monotheism. In reality, the 'Gods' of old should, in Christian terms, be regarded as equivalent to the angelic states, or divine attributes. In some stories the Mother-Goddess has quite rightly been translated as the Virgin, Queen of Heaven. However, in other stories the 'Gods' of old seem to have been translated into 'demons,' probably from a zeal to suppress polytheism and without any understanding that they may be regarded as divine attributes.

Truly great, or inspired literature is characterised by two things: Its use of language, and the plurality of meanings contained in one and the same piece of writing. These old legends can be regarded as great by virtue of the variety of meanings contained within them. Many of them can be taken literally, as stories of love and adventure, but they can also be interpreted from historical, social, psychological, moral, and profoundly esoteric points of view, and no one interpretation excludes any other, each is 'right' in its own sphere.

Because of this plurality of meanings, these legends can appeal to everyone - some seeing them simply as adventure stories, others penetrating to deeper meanings; with them, there is no need of separate 'highbrow' and 'lowbrow' cultures.

The most profound esoteric content of many of these stories refers to man's spiritual quest - the 'lesser mysteries,' leading to a death of the ego and a rebirth as 'True Man' or 'Primordial Man' - and the 'greater mysteries,' leading towards Divine Union. The spiritual pathway may be predominated by action, love, or knowledge, each one suiting different types of person. A few of these stories refer to a way of love, but many of them refer to a way of action. In mediaeval Europe the monasteries in particular provided a way of love and devotion; a way of action was provided, for the aristocrats by knighthood, and for plebeians by the craft initiations. The constantly repeated theme of the spiritual quest, hidden within these stories, no doubt provided an introduction to the esoteric ways existing in the Celtic countries right up to modern times.

A given spiritual pathway also requires virtue, and a method. One of the best-known spiritual methods consists of the repetition of a sacred phrase (in Hinduism, 'Mantra-Yoga,' in Islam, 'Dhikr' or remembrance, in Orthodox Christianity, the 'Prayer of the Heart'). In some of these stories the hero is given a ring - symbol of eternity, or of endless 'remembrance' - representing his method; its loss implying a fall into 'forgetfulness.'

At the end of each part, or section, we have added a brief commentary which is not intended to be exhaustive, covering all points, or possible explanations, but merely to point out something of what the stories are about; other interpretations are possible, and any given one does not necessarily exclude another.

Attitudes to Celtic literature have changed tremendously during modern times. Bullfinch quotes a letter written in 1802 by the poet Southey, addressed to John Rickman Esq: '.....The Mabinogion.....but where did the Cymri get the imagination that could produce such a tale?... I am perfectly astonished that such fictions should exist in Welsh....' The above stands in sharp contrast to present-day acceptance of Celtic culture, underlined by a recent writer's reference to the Mabinogion as 'truth-bearing fiction' (Humphreys).

In translating these stories, we have used some colloquial English for reported speech, but the rest of the text is in fairly formal English, for, to try to translate Luzel's literary French into informal narrative would hardly recapture the rustic and archaic style of the old Breton storytellers. We have used capitals instead of lower case for some words, e.g. 'a Prince,' because the context seemed to require emphasis, 'a Church,' to remind readers this may be an interpolation to a story older than Christianity.

6

PART 1. TRAVELLING TOWARDS THE SUN.

Chapter 1. The Crystal Palace.

Once there were two poor people, husband and wife, who had seven children, six boys and a girl. The youngest boy, Yvon, and the girl, Yvonne, were a little weak-minded, or at least so they seemed, and their brothers caused them all sorts of misery. Poor Yvonne was quite saddened by this, and she almost never laughed. Every morning, her brothers sent her to look after the cows and sheep, on a great heath, with a piece of barley bread or a buckwheat cake as her sole pittance, and she only came back at sunset. One morning when she was leading her cows and sheep to the heath, she met such a handsome and shining young man that she believed she was seeing the Sun in person; and the young man came towards her and said:

- 'Would you like to marry me, young girl?'

Yvonne was too astonished and embarrassed to know what to say.

- 'I don't know,' she said, lowering her eyes, 'they give me a bad enough life at home.'

- 'Well think about it then; I'll be waiting here at the same time tomorrow.'

And then the handsome young man disappeared. All day, the young girl could dream only of him. She went back home at sunset, driving her flock before her and singing merrily. All the others were astonished, and they said to each other:

- 'What's happened to Yvonne, to make her sing like that?'

When she had put her cows and sheep inside, she went up to her mother and told her about her meeting and asked what she should say to him.

- 'Poor fool,' said her mother, 'what kind of a tale is this? And why dream of marrying, only to be more unhappy?'

- 'I'll never be more unhappy than I am now, mother.'

Her mother shrugged her shoulders, and turned her back on her.

Next morning at sunrise, Yvonne went, as usual, to the great heath, with her cows and sheep. At the same place as before, she met the handsome young man, who said again:

- 'Well, young girl, will you be my wife?'

- 'I'd like that very much,' she replied, blushing.

- 'Well then! Let's go back and I'll ask your parents' consent.'

And he went back home with her. The father and mother, and the brothers too, were astonished to see such a fine Prince, so richly dressed, wishing to marry the poor shepherdess, and no one dreamt of saying no.

- 'But who are you?' asked the mother.
- 'You'll know on the wedding-day,' replied the Prince.

They fixed a day for the ceremony, and then the Prince left, leaving them all in the greatest astonishment, and they busied themselves with the wedding preparations.

On the appointed day, the Prince came with a best man almost as handsome as himself. They were in a fine gilded carriage, drawn by four magnificent white horses; and they and their carriage and horses were so adorned and shining that they shone on everything they passed like the sun.

The wedding was celebrated with much pomp and solemnity, and, as soon as he left the table, the Prince told his bride to climb in the carriage, to go to his palace. Yvonne asked for a little time to gather her clothing.

- 'There's no need,' said the Prince, 'you'll find all you could wish for in my palace.'

And she climbed into the carriage, alongside her husband. Just as they were leaving, her brothers asked:

- 'Where can we find our sister, when we want to visit her?'
- 'At the Crystal Palace, on the other side of the Black Sea,' replied the Prince as they left.

About a year later, as the six brothers had no news of their sister, and as they were curious to know how she was getting on with her new husband, they resolved to go in search of her. The five eldest ones mounted fine horses, and set out. Their younger brother Yvon had also wished to go with them, but they had made him stay at home.

They rode and they rode, always towards the rising sun, and they asked everywhere for the Crystal Palace; but no one knew where it was. At last, after having crossed many countries, they came one day to the edge of a great forest which was at least fifty leagues in circumference. They asked an old woodman if he could tell them the way to the Crystal Palace. He replied:

- 'There's a great ride in the forest called Crystal Palace Lane; perhaps it goes there, but I've never been there myself.'

The five brothers went into the forest. They had not gone far, when they heard a great noise above their heads, like a thunder-storm passing over the tree-tops, with thunder and lightning. They were scared, and their horses also, to the point where they had difficulty in restraining them; but the noise and flashes of lightning soon stopped, and they went on their way. Night was approaching, and they were worried, for the forest abounded in all kinds of wild beasts. One of them climbed a tree, to see if he could see the Crystal Palace, or some other dwelling.

- 'Can you see anything?' his brothers asked from below.
- 'Only trees, trees.... everywhere - as far as I can see.'

He climbed down and they continued on their way. But night came upon them and they could no longer see their way. Once more, one of them climbed a tree.

- 'Can you see anything?' asked his brothers.
- 'Yes, there's a big fire, over there!'
- 'Throw your hat in the same direction, and come down.'

And they went in the direction of the fire, believing there must be some human dwelling there; then again they heard a great noise above their heads, louder than the first time. Trees clashed against each other and creaked, and broken branches and splinters of wood fell on all sides. And what thunder!.... What lightning!.... It was terrifying!.... Then, all of a sudden, silence returned and the night became calm and serene.

They continued on their way and reached the fire. A bearded old woman, with long rattling teeth, was busy throwing wood on it. They went up to her, and the eldest brother said:

- 'Good evening, grandmother. Can you tell us the way to the Crystal Palace?'
- 'Yes, truly,' replied the old woman; 'but wait until my eldest son comes back; he goes there every day, and he'll give you the latest news from there. He's away just now, but he'll soon be back. Perhaps you've even seen him in the forest?'
- 'We haven't seen anyone, grandmother.'
- 'But you must have heard him, for one generally hears him when he passes by.... Hold on! Here he comes - can you hear him?'

And they heard an uproar similar to what they had heard twice in the forest, but still more frightening.

- 'Hide yourselves, quickly - there, under the tree branches,' said the old woman, 'for my son's always very hungry when he comes back, and I fear he might eat you.'

The five brothers hid themselves the best they could, and a giant came down from the sky, and, as soon as he touched the ground, he started sniffing and said:

- 'There's a smell of Christians here, mother, and I must eat them, for I'm very hungry.'

The old woman took a large cudgel, and, showing it to the giant, said:

- 'You always want to eat everything, you! But watch out for my cudgel! If you do the slightest harm to my nephews, my sister's sons, such fine and good children, who've come to see me.'

The giant trembled in fear at the old woman's threat, and promised not to harm his cousins.

Then the old woman told the five brothers they could show themselves, and she introduced them to her son, who said:

- 'My cousins are very nice, but aren't they small, mother!'

After all, as they were cousins, he wouldn't want to eat them!

- 'Not only will you not harm them, but you must also do them a favour,' said the mother.

- 'What sort of favour must I do for them?'

- 'They want to go and see their sister at the Crystal Palace, and you must lead them there.'

- 'I can't lead them that far, but I'll willingly lead them a good way, and set them on the right road.'

- 'Thanks cousin, we couldn't ask for more,' they said.

- 'Well now! Lie down by the fire and sleep, for we must be off early in the morning. I'll wake you when it's time.'

The five brothers lay down in their overcoats and pretended to sleep; they could not sleep, for they had not too much confidence in the giant's promise. The latter ate his supper, and he swallowed a whole sheep with every mouthful.

Towards midnight, he woke the five brothers, and said:

- 'Let's go! Get up, cousins; it's time to leave.'

He spread a large black sheet on the ground, near the fire, and told the five brothers to go on it mounted on their horses. Then the giant went into the fire, and his mother threw wood on it. As the fire steadily increased, they heard a gradually increasing noise, like the one they had heard in the forest, and, little by little, the sheet lifted the brothers and their horses off the ground. When the giant's clothing was consumed, he rose up in the air as an enormous ball of fire. The black sheet followed, carrying the brothers and their horses through the air. After some time they landed on a great plain. Half of this plain was arid and burnt, the other half was fertile and covered in thick, tall grass. There was a herd of shiny, strong horses on the arid part; where the grass was thick and tall, there was, on the contrary, a herd of horses so thin and emaciated they could scarcely stand on their feet, and they were fighting and trying to eat one another.

The giant, or the ball of fire, had continued on his way, after having said to the brothers: 'Now you're on the right road for the Crystal Palace; do your best from now on, for I can't take you any further.'

Their horses had died on touching the ground, so they were now on foot. First of all, they each tried to catch one of the fine horses from the arid part of the plain; but they were unable to do so. Then they tried the emaciated horses which they were each able to catch and mount; but the horses took them amongst the gorse and scrub which covered part of the plain, and threw them, all cut and bleeding. They were in a mess! What should they do? - 'Let's go back home, we'll never reach this accursed palace,' said one of them.

- 'In fact, there's nothing else we can do,' replied the others.

And they retraced their steps, but they avoided the spot where they had met the old woman tending the fire, and her giant son.

At last they returned home, after much toil and trouble, and told all that had happened on their travels. Yvon was, as usual, sitting on a round stone in a corner by the fire; when he had heard the story of all their troubles, he said:

- 'I also want to try this adventure. It's my turn, and I won't come back until I've seen my sister, Yvonne.'

- 'You imbecile,' said his brothers, shrugging their shoulders.

- 'Yes me, and I'll find her, I tell you, wherever she is.'

They gave him an old, worn-out horse and he set out alone.

He followed the same route as his brothers, always travelling in the direction of the rising sun, reached the forest, and, at the entrance to Crystal Palace Lane, he met an old woman, who said:

- 'Where are you going like that, young man?'

- 'To the Crystal Palace, grandmother, to see my sister.'

- 'In that case, don't take this road, but follow that one until you reach a great plain; then, you follow the edge of the plain, until you see a road made of black earth. Take that road, and, whatever happens, whatever you see or hear, even if the road is full of fire, always keep going straight ahead, fearlessly, and you'll reach the Crystal Palace and see your sister.'

- 'Thank you, grandmother,' replied Yvon, and he started out along the way the old woman had indicated.

He reached the plain without delay, and went along the edge until he saw the road of black earth. He wanted to take the latter, but the entrance was full of writhing snakes, so he was afraid and hesitated for a moment. When he tried to go in, his horse withdrew in horror. 'What should I do?' he said, 'for I've been told this is the way.'

He drove his spurs into his horse's flanks and went forward, but straight away the snakes wrapped themselves around the animal's legs, bit it, and it fell dead on the spot. Poor Yvon was on foot in the midst of these hideous reptiles, which hissed and poised themselves menacingly around him. But he did not lose his courage for that; he walked on, and at last reached the other end of the road unharmed. His fear left him.

He found himself on the edge of a great lake; he could not see any boat, and he could not swim. - 'What should I do?' he said to himself; 'I don't want to retrace my footsteps; I'll try to get across, come what may.'

And he went resolutely into the water. First it came up to his knees, then his armpits, then his chin, and finally above his head. He kept going forwards, despite all, and ended up, unharmed, on the other side of the lake.

On leaving the water, he found himself at the beginning of a deep path, narrow and dark and full of thorns and brambles which stretched right across, rooted on both sides.

- 'I'll never get through there,' he thought; but he did not give up; he crawled on all-fours beneath the brambles, slid like a snake, and managed to get through. What a mess he was; his skin was torn and bleeding, and there was not a stitch of clothing left on him. But he had done it, despite all.

A little further on, he saw a thin, emaciated horse galloping towards him. It came close, stopped as if to invite him to mount, and he recognised it as his own, which he had believed was dead. He showed great joy at finding it alive, and climbed on its back saying: 'A thousand blessings on you, for I'm too tired to walk any further.'

They continued on their way and came to a place where there was a large stone resting on two others. The horse struck its hoof on the upper stone, which tilted exposing a tunnel entrance, and a voice from within said: 'Get off your horse, and come in.'

He obeyed the voice and went into the tunnel. At first he was suffocated by an unbearable smell of venomous reptiles. Moreover the tunnel was so dark he could only grope his way forward. After a few moments he heard a frightful din behind him, sounding like a legion of demons coming towards him. 'No doubt I shall die here,' he thought. He carried on as best he could and eventually saw a glimmer of light ahead, which gave him hope. The noise behind him was getting closer; but the light was getting brighter also. At last, he came out of the tunnel safe and sound.....

Then he found himself at a cross roads. Which road should he take? He followed the one opposite the tunnel exit, and kept going straight ahead. There were many high gates across this road. He was unable to open them, and climbed up the posts and over the tops. The road went downhill, and at the far end every-thing appeared to be made of crystal. He saw a crystal palace, a crystal sky, a crystal sun, in short everything he saw was in crystal. - 'They said my sister lives in a crystal palace; I must be near the end of my journey and troubles, for it really exists,' he said happily.

When he reached the Crystal Palace, it was so resplendent with light that his eyes were dazzled. He went into the court-yard and everything was shining. He saw a large number of doors, but they were all locked. He managed to slide into a cellar, through a ventilation shaft, and from there he went up and found himself in a great hall, magnificent and resplendent with light. Six doors opened into this hall, and they opened them-selves as soon as he touched them. From this first hall, he went into a second, even more beautiful. Three other doors there open-ed into three other halls of increasing beauty. In the last hall, he saw his sister asleep on a fine bed. He spent some time look-ing at her, rooted to the spot in admiration, so beautiful did he find her. But she did not wake up, and evening came. Then he heard footsteps coming, with a sound of spherical bells at each step. Then a fine young man came in, went straight to Yvonne's bed, and gave her three resounding slaps. Despite that, she neither woke up nor budged. Then the young man lay on the bed by her side. Yvon was quite embarrassed, not sure whether to stay or go away. He decided to stay, for it seemed to him that this young man treated his sister in a strange way. The young husband went to sleep by his wife's side. What astonished Yvon still more, was that he did not hear the slightest sound in the palace, and it seemed they did not eat there. He had arrived with a great appetite; now he had none at all. Night passed in the most profound silence. At daybreak, Yvonne's husband woke up and gave his wife three good slaps, but she did not seem to notice and still did not wake up; then he left directly.

All this astounded Yvon, still silent in his corner. He feared his sister might be dead. At last he decided to assure himself by giving her a kiss; then she woke up, opened her eyes and, seeing her brother next to her, exclaimed:
- 'Oh, what happiness to see you again, brother.'
And they embraced each other tenderly. Then Yvon asked:
- 'And where's your husband?'
- 'He's gone on his travels.'

- 'Has he been away for long?'
- 'No, truly, he's just left, a moment ago.'
- 'Poor sister, why aren't you happy with him?'
- 'But I'm very happy with him.'
- 'But I saw him give you three good slaps last night, when he came in, and again this morning.'
- 'What are you saying, brother? Slaps!.... He kisses me every night and morning.'
- 'Strange kisses to me, really! But after all, seeing you don't complain.... How is it no one eats here?'
- 'Since I've been here, I've never felt hungry, nor thirsty, nor hot, nor cold, nor any need, nor experienced anything unpleasant. Are you hungry yourself?'
- 'No, truly, and it surprises me. Are you and your husband the only ones in this palace?'
- 'No! There are many here. When I first came I saw them all; but I've never seen them since, for I spoke to them, although I'd been told not to.'

They spent the day together, walking around the palace and chatting about their family, their country, and other things. In the evening Yvonne's husband arrived at his usual time. He recognised his brother-in-law and was pleased to see him.

- 'Brother-in-law, you've come to see us, then?' he said.
- 'Yes, and not without a lot of trouble.'
- 'I can believe that, for not anyone can come this far; but you'll go back more easily; I'll see you through the bad parts.'

Yvon stayed several days with his sister. His brother-in-law left every morning, without saying where he was going, and was away all day. Yvon, intrigued by this, asked his sister:

- 'Where does your husband go, every day? What does he do?'
- 'I don't know, he's never told me and I've never asked.'
- 'Well, I feel like asking him if he'll let me go with him, for I'm curious to know where he goes every day.'
- 'Yes, ask him, brother.'

Next morning, just as Yvonne's husband was about to leave, Yvon said to him:

- 'Brother-in-law, I'd like to go with you on your rounds today, to see the country and get some fresh air.'
- 'I'd like that very much, but on condition you do as I say.'
- 'I promise to do everything you say.'
- 'Listen to me carefully, then; above all else you must not touch anything, and speak only to me, whatever you see or hear.'
- 'That's fine; let's go then.'

14

The Crystal Palace.

And they left the Crystal Palace and went along a path so narrow that Yvon had to walk behind Yvonne's husband. Then they came to a great arid, sandy plain where Yvon was surprised to see fat, shiny cattle sitting on the sand, chewing their cud peacefully; yet he did not say a word.

Further on they came to another plain where the grass was thick and tall, yet the cattle there were emaciated, fighting each other and bellowing. Yvon found this strange, and asked:

- 'I've never seen anything like this; cattle thriving on sand, and others almost starving on good pasture. What does it mean?'

- 'The fat shiny cattle on the sand are poor people, who, content with their lot, do not covet others' goods; the thin, starving cattle, always fighting, are the rich who're never satisfied and are always fighting and seeking more at others' expense.'

Further on, by a river bank, they saw two trees clashing and banging against each other so bitterly that splinters of wood were flying far and wide. Yvon was carrying a staff, and when he was close he held it between them, saying:

- 'Why must you mistreat one another like that? Stop hurting one another, and live in peace.'

He had scarcely spoken these words when the trees changed into humans, husband and wife, and said:

- 'Bless you! We've been fighting like this for three hundred years, and no one's had pity on us and deigned to speak a word to us. When we were a couple on earth we argued and fought all the time, and as a punishment, God had condemned us to fight here until some charitable soul should pity us and say a good word to us. You've put an end to our suffering, and now we're going to Paradise where we hope to see you one day.'

And the two disappeared there and then.

Then Yvon heard a terrible uproar, of cries, curses, yells, of gnashing teeth, of dragging chains..... It was enough to freeze the blood in one's veins.

- 'What's going on here?' he asked his brother-in-law.

- 'Now we're at the entrance to Hell; but we can't go any further together, because you've disobeyed me. You've spoken to the two trees, although I strongly advised you not to touch or speak to anyone other than me. Go back to your sister; I'll go on alone. When I get back, I'll put you on the right road for home.'

And Yvon went back to the Crystal Palace, alone and quite upset, whilst his brother-in-law went on his way.

When his sister saw him, she said:

- 'What! You're back already?'

15

- 'Yes dear,' he replied sadly.
- 'And you've come back alone?'
- 'Yes, all alone.'
- 'You must have disobeyed my husband?'
- 'Yes, I spoke to two trees which were fighting bitterly, and your husband told me to go back to the palace.'
- 'So you still don't know where he goes?'
- 'No, I still don't know.'

Yvonne's husband came back at his usual time, and said:
- 'You disobeyed me, brother-in-law; you broke your promise, and now you must go back to your own country for a short while; you'll come back here soon, and then it'll be for always.'

Yvon said his good-byes to his sister. His brother-in-law put him on the right road, and said:
- 'Now go without fear, and *au revoir*, for you'll soon be back.'

Yvon followed the road, a little sad at returning thus, and nothing hindered him on his journey. What surprised him even more, was that he was neither hungry, nor thirsty, nor needing sleep. By dint of walking without ever stopping, neither by day nor at night - for he no longer became tired - he at last reached his country. He went to the place where he expected to find his father's house, and was quite astonished to find a field there, with very old beeches and oaks.
- 'This is the spot, or I'm very mistaken,' he said to himself.

He went into a house, not far away, and asked where Iouenn Dagorn, his father, lived.
- 'Iouenn Dagorn?... There's no one by that name,' they replied.

However an old man, who was sitting in the ingle-nook, said:
- 'I've heard my grandfather speak of an Iouenn Dagorn; but he's been dead a long time, and his children and grandchildren also, and there are no more Dagorns in the land.'

Poor Yvon could not have been more astonished by what he heard, and, as he no longer knew anyone in the land and no one knew him, he told himself there was nothing left there for him, and that the best thing would be to follow his family to where they had gone. He went to the cemetery and saw their graves, some of which already dated from three hundred years ago. Then he went into the Church, and prayed from the bottom of his heart, dying there and then, and going, no doubt, to rejoin his sister in the Crystal Palace.

(Told by Louis Le Braz, weaver, Prat [Côtes-du-Nord] 1873).

Commentary.

Luzel gave a number of stories under the heading of 'Travelling towards the Sun,' from which we have selected the story of the Crystal Palace.

Although it can be taken literally, as an adventure story into another world, this story is esoteric and its main theme is the spiritual quest, symbolised as a journey in search of a sister who is married to the Sun, or Sun-God. The 'sister' may be interpreted as representing man's inner spirit, with whom he has lost contact through worldliness; the Sun, in monotheistic terms, may be interpreted as representing Divine Majesty. This story is without doubt of ancient, pre-Christian origin.

Yvonne's five brothers set out on the journey to the Crystal Palace - the journey of the 'lesser mysteries' - and, after some frightening experiences, they meet the Mother-Goddess in the guise of a repulsive old hag. They have some virtue, for they greet her with respect, and she, in return, protects them. In this part of the story, the Sun manifests himself as a hideous giant, very hungry on his return home, and with an appetite for 'Christians' (probably 'men' in an earlier version). Divine Majesty, represented here as the Sun, has two aspects: one burning, wrathful and consuming, and represented by the giant; the other splendid, shining and beneficent, represented by the form of Yvonne's husband. Just as an object passing too close to the sun would be burnt, so mortals who were spiritually 'unqualified' would be consumed by a direct approach to Divine Majesty, unless they had some protection, in this case, that of the Mother-Goddess. One does not have to look far in the history books to find analogous examples of royal, or imperial courts where plebeian intruders would risk punishment or death, unless they were properly presented and under the protection of a courtier. The intervention of the Mother-Goddess permits the brothers to continue their quest, with some help from her son, but they soon give up.

Yvonne's brother Yvon, ignoring his brothers' derision, sets out with great determination. He is given advice on which road to take through the forest to avoid the Sun's wrathful aspect. He reaches the Crystal Palace only after a long, hazardous and difficult journey. This journey represents the first part of the spiritual quest, the accomplishment of the 'lesser mysteries,' and his brother-in-law tells him that not all mortals can go that far. The story makes it clear that many of the hazards encountered on that journey, across the psychic 'other world,' are illusions - the snakes appearing to kill his horse, the lake in which he was not drowned, etc. Nonetheless they are real for Yvon at the time, and only seen as illusions later.

Yvon sets out, with Yvonne's husband as guide, on the second part of the spiritual quest - the 'greater mysteries' - but fails to go far, by breaking the rules - disobeying his guide and spiritual master. He was distracted by what he saw, intervened, and spoke.

The story also points out that values, and the order of things, are different in states or modes of existence other than this earthly corporeal one. This is emphasised by representing slaps as kisses, and by Yvon's brief stay in the Crystal Palace representing about three hundred years on earth.

The description of the cattle on the plain may be interpreted as representing the true interior condition of people as they are in this life; it is generally interpreted as representing Purgatory, but the pre-Christian and early Celtic Christian Traditions envisaged a wider notion of posthumous possibilities than Heaven, Hell, and Purgatory, including reincarnation. Although one modern commentator, Markale, is of the opinion that the Celts did not believe in reincarnation, Taliesin's poem seems to affirm the contrary:

'...................I have been in Asia with Noah in the ark,
I have seen the destruction of Sodom and Gomorrah....'

At the end, the poet affirms that now he is Taliesin! Although Taliesin was writing in the sixth century, that is to say in the Christian era, his work embodies much from the Old Tradition, and in some ways forms a 'bridge' between the two. It is only right to point out that Markale's comment was in the context of discussing interpretations of shamanistic metamorphoses of men into animal forms; we agree with him that the latter should not be interpreted as representing reincarnation. Readers wishing to look further into this question of reincarnation may consult the book by Head and Cranston.

In this story the colour black should be regarded as representing mystery; no geographical significance should be given to the Black Sea, it should be interpreted as the sea of mystery; likewise the black sheet, and the road of black earth.

PART 2. THE FAITHFUL SERVANT.

Chapter 2. King Dalmar.

You should know
How it once was.....

Once there was a King of France who had a son. When the latter became a young man, he told his father he wished to marry.

- 'Whom do you wish to marry, son?'
- 'King Dalmar's daughter.'
- 'Alas my boy, you can never have her. Since she was twelve years old, she's been locked in a tower, and no one ever visits her except the woman who takes her food every day.'
- 'I'm not put off by that, I can always go and ask her father, for if I can't have her as my wife, I'll have no one else. I don't know which way to go to find King Dalmar's court; but by dint of travelling, I'll end up there sooner or later.'
- 'If you're so resolved, I'll not oppose you; but you must be back here within a year and a day.'
- 'I promise you that.'

And he left in a fine carriage, accompanied only by a man-servant. They went haphazardly, not knowing which direction to take. They kept on going forwards, without ever stopping. One day they were caught out at night in the middle of a forest. The horses were tired, and the servant suggested they unharness them, to give them some rest, and spend the night in the forest. The Prince agreed. He slept, as usual, in his carriage, and the servant stretched out on the moss and bracken at the foot of an old oak, close to the horses.

Towards midnight, the servant heard a noise above his head, like a great bird alighting to spend the night in the tree. He raised his head and saw, in the moonlight, someone sitting in an armchair balanced on the branches. This surprised him greatly. A moment later, he heard a second noise, and a second person came and sat in a second armchair; then, a third. The first one started the conversation, saying:

- 'Well! Have you had a good day? Have you any news?'
- 'It's been a bad day, and we've no news,' replied the others.
- 'Well, I know something new. The son of the King of France is in the woods.'
- 'Really? What a windfall; if we could get our hands on him.'
- 'He's going to ask for the hand of King Dalmar's daughter; but he's not yet at the end of his troubles; it won't be as easy

as he thinks, to reach King Dalmar's court. When he leaves the forest, he'll come to a river, sixty leagues wide. How will he cross it when there's neither ferry nor boat to be found? There's just one way, and if he'd been here, I could have told him.'

The Prince's servant pricked up his ears, as well you might believe.

- 'And what way is there?' asked the two others.

- 'When he reaches the river, he should cut a wand from the hedge on the side of the rising sun, remove the bark, and then strike the water with it three times. Straight away a fine bridge will rise up from the river; he'll be able to cross and reach King Dalmar's capital easily; but that's not all; when he reaches the city, he'll have to disguise himself as a Princess and present himself to the King as a friend of his daughter, whom she would have known in Spain, and who has come to visit her. He should ask to sleep in the same room as the King's daughter, and he'd be able to take her out through the window at night. If he'd been here to listen to me, he could have benefited from this advice, and perhaps succeeded in his enterprise.'

Just then, day began to break, and the three flew off.

The servant had heard it all, but he said nothing to his master. He woke the latter, who had been sleeping all night, and had heard nothing; he harnessed the horses and they set out; soon they caught sight of the river.

- 'Alas, we'll have to stop here,' said the Prince when he saw such a great expanse of water.

- 'Perhaps, Master; but don't give up,' said the servant.

- 'And how do you think we'll get across? It won't be by swimming, I think; and there's no ferry and no sign of a boat.'

The servant said nothing. He went to the hedge on the side of the rising sun, cut a hazel wand with his knife and started removing the bark, whilst continuing on their way. When they reached the river, he struck the water three times with his wand and immediately they saw a fine bridge rise up, reaching from one side to the other.

- 'What kind of man are you?' said the Prince, astonished.

They crossed the river with ease, and soon they were in King Dalmar's capital. They went to the best hotel in town.

Next morning, the servant said to his master:

- 'Now you must disguise yourself as a Princess and go to see King Dalmar, telling him you knew his daughter in Spain, and that you've come to spend a few days with her. You'll also insist on staying with the Princess day and night, and even sleeping in her room. The King will readily agree to your request. Take a rope with you, under your dress. At midnight, when everyone's asleep, I'll be beneath your window with the carriage, and you and the Princess can come down and we'll leave at once.'

The Prince had limitless confidence in his servant, since the river crossing, and he did everything he said. He went to the castle disguised as a Princess, and asked to speak to the King.

- 'Greetings, King Dalmar,' he said.
- 'Greetings, young Princess,' replied the King.
- 'I'm a friend of your daughter; I knew her in Spain and I've come to spend a few days with her.'
- 'Welcome! I'll call my daughter, she'll be pleased to see you.'

And he had his daughter brought, and left the two of them together, alone. They easily got permission to spend the night in the same room. Then the Prince told her who he was, explaining the reason for his visit and his disguise, and asked her if she would follow him.

- 'I'll follow you wherever you wish,' she replied; 'my father keeps me locked up in this tower all the time; I never see anyone and I'm anxious to recover my freedom.'

At midnight they were ready to leave, and through the window they heard the Prince's servant saying:

- 'Get ready to come down; tie the rope and throw it to me.'

They did so, but, just as they were about to go down, the Princess took fright and said:

- 'Alas, poor Prince, my father's a magician; he'll soon know that we've gone and send his soldiers after us. It'll be bad for us if we're captured.'
- 'Let's go anyway,' replied the Prince, 'we'll see what happens later.'

They went down the rope, climbed into the waiting carriage, and left at a triple gallop.

- 'Alas, I can hear my father's soldiers coming,' cried the Princess after some time.

And in fact, they were coming at a fast gallop, with the King at their head. They were going to catch up with them, the soldiers were on the bridge over the river which marked the boundary of King Dalmar's kingdom. As soon as the Prince reached the other side, his servant struck the bridge three times with his wand, and it fell into the water. All were drowned, except for King Dalmar himself, who, from the other side of the river shook his fist and cried out in anger:

- 'You've wronged me, son of France; but before you get to Paris with my daughter, you'll have me to contend with again.'

However the Prince and Princess, now free from all care, went peacefully on their way. Night came upon them in the same woods, and, on the servant's advice, they decided to wait there until daylight. The Prince and Princess slept in the carriage, and the servant stretched out at the foot of the same tree as before. At midnight, once again he heard the sound of wings, like great birds coming to rest in the tree, and then a voice said:

- 'Are we all here?'

- 'Yes,' replied another voice, 'except for the Lame Devil, but he's always late, as well you know.'

The Lame Devil came also, a moment later.

- 'Well, what's new?' the others asked him.

- 'What's new? Then don't you know? The son of the King of France is in the woods again. He's managed to get Princess Dalmar, and he's taking her to Paris. But he'll have trouble before he gets there. First of all, when he leaves the woods, he'll be attacked by twelve thieves and they'll take all their gold, their carriage, and even their clothing. They'll leave them all naked, just as they came into the world; and if any of them offers resistance, he'll be changed straight away into marble. In this sorry state, they'll meet an old woman on the threshold of a thatched cottage; she'll invite them to go in and accept some clothing. If they're unfortunate enough to go in and accept some clothing from her - for she'll have plenty to choose from - straight away they'll be changed into marble statues, and they'll come to warm themselves at our place. Then they'll come to a lake, in which they'll see a man about to drown and calling for help; hard luck for them if they help him, for they'll be transformed instantly into marble statues. That's all the trials they'll have to suffer before reaching Paris. And how do you think they'll come out of it? They'd only be able to do so if someone were to tell them what I've just told you, and none of you are daft enough to do that; on the other hand, no one can hear our conversation here; and even if someone could hear it, if he were to tell the Prince before a year and a day, he'd immediately be changed into a marble statue, and come straight to us to warm himself.'

Day began to break, and those who were on the tree left, or rather, flew away.

The servant, lying under the tree, had heard everything. He woke his master, but said nothing to him, harnessed the horses, and they set off. They had scarcely left the wood when twelve thieves threw themselves on them, stopping their horses, and shouting 'your money or your life.' They forced the Prince and Princess out of the carriage, took all their clothes off them, the servant's as well, and then they left, taking the carriage and horses with them. Our people, left naked like savages, no longer dared show themselves on the road in daylight. They hid themselves in the woods, and travelled at night. An old woman saw them passing by her thatched cottage, and called out:

- 'Jesus! Whatever's happened to you poor folk? What a state to see Christians in! Come inside and I'll give you some clothing; I won't let you go like that.'

The Prince and Princess wanted to go in; the servant did all he could to prevent them; but in vain; they went into the old woman's house. Then the servant set fire to the house, forcing them to come out before they had had time to put any clothes on. They were not amused. They had to carry on again in this pitiful state. The servant found some old trousers, no doubt fallen from some rag merchant's bag. He put them on, and could then go to the surrounding farms begging for bread and pancakes for all of them. They came like that to the edge of a great lake, where they saw a man on the point of drowning, and who was calling pitifully for help.

The Prince wanted to throw himself in the water to save this man. It took the servant all his time to stop him. He went to the water's edge and beat the drowning man on the head with his wand until he disappeared beneath the water.

- 'You're wicked,' said the Prince and Princess to him; 'you've let this man die, when you could have saved him.'

But the servant took little notice of this reproach, and they went on their way.

They were getting close to Paris. The servant, who had his trousers, went before them into the town and brought them some clothes back. Then they could show themselves decently, and all three of them went to the King's palace together. The old monarch, who believed his son dead, celebrated his return by public rejoicing.

Some time later, the Prince married King Dalmar's daughter, and again there was feasting and rejoicing.

Nine or ten months after the wedding, a son was born, bringing their happiness to its height.

The Prince had kept his faithful servant, and often they spoke together of their extraordinary adventure. He was most intrigued to know how he had been able to get them out of all the difficult spots they had been in, and often questioned him about it.

- 'I'll tell you,' replied the servant, 'but only when it's the right time; I can't do so at present.'

The Prince's desire and curiosity only increased with this resistance, and he pressed more and more; but always in vain. In the end, he went furiously into the servant's room, sword in hand, and cried out:

- 'Tell me your secret, or I'll kill you here and now.'
- 'I'll tell you, Master, since you order me to; but you'll regret it later.'
- 'Speak, I tell you, or get ready to die.'

And he brandished his broad sword above his head.

- 'Do you recall the night we slept in the woods on the way to King Dalmar's?'
- 'Yes,' replied the Prince.
- 'You slept in the carriage, but I spent the night at the foot of an old tree. Towards midnight I heard voices in the tree; there were three persons who gave me the impression they were demons. One of them, no doubt unaware that I was there, told the others of our presence in the woods, the aim of our journey and what must be done for it to succeed.'

Already the faithful servant's feet had turned to marble. His master saw it clearly, but he let him go on:

- 'On the way back we spent the night in the same woods. The same thing happened, and I learnt what had to be done on the return journey to arrive safely at your father's palace.'

The Prince, seeing his faithful servant already turned to marble up to the waist, exclaimed:

- 'Enough! Enough! Don't go any further.'
- 'No, seeing I've started, I must go on to the end. I hadn't to tell you this secret, under pain of being turned to marble. You ordered me to speak; you are my Master; I obeyed you; now you know everything and the prediction has come true.'

And now the faithful servant had become a marble statue. His last words were:

- 'Now I'm done for; I'm going to burn in hell-fire, and you'll come to join me there, if you don't redeem your sin.'

The Prince was inconsolable over his servant's misfortune. He became sad and kept away from people, and he was often seen weeping. No one, not even his wife, knew what had made him change so.

One day, his old father asked him:

- 'Where's that faithful servant you like so much? I haven't seen him for some time.'

The Prince remained silent.

- 'I hope you haven't put him to death.'
- 'No, father, I assure you I haven't done that.'

All the time he was thinking of what he should do, whom he should ask for advice. After having consulted many learned men in vain, including magicians and wizards, he got the idea of spending a night in the forest, at the same place as before. He set out in his carriage one morning, without telling anyone where he was going, and went to the forest. He found the spot without trouble, and lay down beneath the tree, but he did not sleep. At midnight he heard a flapping of great wings above his head, and then a voice which said:

- 'Well comrades, the Prince's servant's come to warm himself at our place, just like I said; and the Prince will come also, without much delay, I hope. There's only one way for him to avoid it, and restore his faithful servant.'

The Prince was all ears, as you might well believe. The other one said:

- 'He'll have to cut his only son's throat during the high mass, collect all the blood in a vase and sprinkle it over the marble statue that was his servant, and then pour this same blood back into his son's mouth and lie him in his cradle. Little by little the statue will come back to life as the blood's sprinkled on it, and, before the end of the high mass, the servant will be completely returned to his original state; the child will also resuscitate soon after, and will be just as it was before. That's what he'll have to do; but how do you think he'll ever get the idea of it?'

Day began to break, and the tree's guests flew off with a great flapping of wings.

The Prince had taken in every word they had spoken. He went back home a little less sad, and full of hope.

The following Sunday he told all his people to go to the high mass, and to leave him alone at home. They all went, and he was absolutely alone in the palace. When he heard the bells tolling for the beginning of the high mass, he took a knife and went resolutely towards the cradle where his son was sleeping.

But his courage left him just as he was about to strike, and he withdrew in horror and started crying.

A moment later he went back with greater resolution; he turned the head to one side and struck. The blood flowed at once.

The Faithful Servant.

He collected it in a vase, ran to the statue, and began rubbing his son's warm blood over it. As he rubbed, he saw the marble coming back to life, and, just as the mass was ending, the statue walked and the faithful servant spoke as follows:

- 'Ah, how hot I've been! I was told I'd be hot if I revealed the secret, and it wasn't a lie. The same would have happened to you, if you hadn't done something about it; but don't waste any time; put the blood back in your son's mouth, and don't worry.'

The Prince hurried to do as he had said, but he was not free from worry. Soon after, his people came back from the high mass. They sat down to eat, as usual. The Princess and the old King were surprised to see their faithful servant back, and they could not understand why the Prince looked more worried than ever.

- 'Where's the child?' asked the Princess.
- 'In his cradle, and he's sleeping soundly,' he replied.

A moment later they heard a cry, like that of a child waking up; he got up from the table, ran to the room, and came back straight away holding him in his arms, wide awake and smiling at his mother. Then he told them the whole story.

Then there was feasting and rejoicing in the palace. I myself slipped by the crowd of servants and went to the kitchen; but, as I dipped my fingers in all the sauces, the master-chef gave me a great kick which sent me right here to tell you my story.

(Told by Jean le Person, shoemaker, village of Plouaret, 1869).

The Faithful Servant.

Commentary.

This story contains three elements: the Prince's quest, the faithful servant, and the near-sacrifice of the Prince's son.

The Prince sets out on a quest, or adventure, in search of a Princess held prisoner in 'another world' by a Magician-King. The boundary between this, and the other - psychic - world is marked by an expanse of water. The Prince outwits the Magician-King and returns home with a 'treasure,' the Princess. All this is classical. From the point of view of interior symbolism, the Princess represents the spirit hidden within man's 'heart;' King Dalmar represents the ego, and his power, man's worldliness and vices which prevent him from knowing the 'spirit within himself.' The accomplishment of the 'lesser mysteries' represented by this quest - the return to 'True Man' or 'Primordial Man,' involves a death (of the ego) and a re-birth - hence the trio's nakedness on the return journey.

The faithful servant obtains secret knowledge permitting him to advise and assist the Prince through the hazardous parts of his quest. The servant is punished for revealing the secret of his knowledge. - All this is understandable, except that the servant receives his knowledge from 'demons,' for all the traditions warn that the latter are jealous of the human race, and their advice is not to be trusted. It might be argued that the servant overhears the demons' conversation without their knowing it, but in another version - 'The King of Portugal' - the 'Lame Devil' calls out 'listen,' clearly indicating that he intends the conversation to be overheard. In one of Grimm's tales, a faithful servant is punished for having revealed the secret of the birds' conversation! One is left wondering if it were originally a question of the 'secret of the Gods,' and that the latter have been changed into 'demons' during the Christian epoch? Stories of people being changed into marble occur elsewhere; they may be taken literally, or, perhaps, as implying a form of paralysis.

The near-sacrifice in the last part of the story is reminiscent of Abraham's; the father has to accept the sacrifice mentally, but it does not have to be carried out in the literal sense. In this story, we must assume that the act of sacrifice took place in a dream, vision, or other analogous psychic state, but not in the corporeal state, or literal sense, so that the child was unharmed.

PART 3. SEEKING THE GOLDEN-HAIRED PRINCESS.

Chapter 3. N'oun-Doaré.

A long time ago,
When chickens had teeth.

One day, when the Marquis of Coat-Squiriou was returning from Morlaix, accompanied by a servant, he saw a four or five-year-old child lying asleep in the roadside ditch. He dismounted, woke up the child, and said:
- 'What are you doing there, child?'
- 'I don't know,' he replied.
- 'Who's your father?'
- 'I don't know.'
- 'And your mother?'
- 'I don't know.'
- 'Where do you come from?'
- 'I don't know.'
- 'What's your name?'
- 'I don't know,' he kept on answering.

The Marquis told his servant to take him on the crupper of his horse, and they went on their way to Coat-Squiriou.

The child was named N'oun-Doaré, which means 'I don't know,' in Breton.

They sent him to school at Carhaix, and he learnt all they taught him.

When he was twenty, the Marquis said to him:
- 'Now you're educated enough, and you should come with me to Coat-Squiriou.'

And he took him there.

On the fourteenth of October, the Marquis and N'oun-Doaré went together to the big fair at Morlaix, and they went to the best inn.

- 'I'm pleased with you,' said the Marquis to the young man.

And they went together to an armourer's and looked at many a good sword; but none of them pleased him, and they left without having bought anything. Whilst they were passing a scrap-metal dealer's shop, N'oun-Doaré stopped, saw a rusty old sword, seized it and exclaimed:

'This is the sword for me!'

- 'What! Look what a state it's in,' said the Marquis; 'it's good for nothing.'

- 'Buy it for me just as it is, please, and you'll see later that it's good for something.'

28

N'oun-Doaré.

The Marquis paid for the rusty old sword, which did not cost him very much, and N'oun-Doaré took it with him, very happy with his acquisition; then they went back to Coat-Squiriou.

The next day, N'oun-Doaré was looking at his sword, when he made out some worn lettering under the rust, which he managed to decipher. It read: 'I am invincible!'

- 'Fantastic!' said N'oun-Doaré to himself.

Some time later, the Marquis said to him:

- 'I should also buy you a horse.'

And they went together to Morlaix, on a fair-day.

There they were on the fair-ground. Certainly there were fine horses from Léon, Tréguier, and Cornwall. And yet, N'oun-Doaré didn't find one to suit him, so that by evening, after sunset, they left the fair-ground without having bought anything.

On their way back, along Saint Nicholas Way, they met a Cornishman leading an old worn-out mare by a rope halter. It was thin like the Mare of Doom. N'oun-Doare stopped, looked at it, and exclaimed:

- 'That's the mare for me!'

- 'What! That sorry steed? But just look at her,' said the Marquis.

- 'Yes, she's the one I want, and no other; buy her for me, please.'

And the Marquis bought the old mare for N'oun-Doaré, protesting at the same time that he had strange tastes.

Whilst handing over his mare, the Cornishman whispered in N'oun-Doaré's ear:

- 'See these knots on the mare's halter?'

- 'Yes,' he replied.

- 'Well, each time you untie one, the mare will straight away transport you fifteen hundred leagues from where you are.'

- 'Tremendous,' he replied.

Then N'oun-Doaré and the Marquis went on their way to Coat-Squiriou, with the old mare. Once there, N'oun-Doaré undid a knot on the halter, and the mare transported him there and then through the air fifteen hundred leagues away. They alighted in the centre of Paris*.

Some months later, the Marquis of Coat-Squiriou came also to Paris, and met N'oun-Doaré by chance.

- 'What a surprise! Have you been here long?' he asked him.

- 'But of course,' he replied.

*The sense of distance was a little lacking in my storyteller.

- 'Then how did you get here?'

And he told him how he had come to Paris so quickly.

They went together to greet the King in his palace. The King knew the Marquis of Coat-squiriou, and gave them a warm welcome.

One moonlit night, N'oun-Doaré went out alone on his old mare, outside the town. He noticed something shining at the foot of an old stone cross, at a cross roads. He approached it, and saw that it was a diamond-studded golden crown.

- 'I'll take it under my coat,' he said to himself.

- 'Take care, or you'll regret it,' said a voice coming from he-didn't-know-where. This voice, which was his mare's, repeated itself three times. He hesitated for a while, but ended up taking the crown away under his coat.

The King had entrusted him to look after some of his horses, and, at night, he used the crown to light his stable, for the diamonds shone in the darkness. His horses were in better condition than those of the other grooms, and the King had often congratulated him, so they were jealous of him. It was expressly forbidden to have a light in the stables at night. When they saw there was always one in N'oun-Doaré's stable, they went and denounced him before the King. At first, the King thought nothing of it, but when they repeated it several times, he asked the Marquis of Coat-Squiriou if there was any truth in it.

- 'I don't know,' replied the Marquis, 'but I'll find out from my servant.'

- 'It's my rusty old sword,' replied N'oun-Doaré, 'which shines in the darkness, for it's a fairy sword.'

But one night his enemies, peeping through the keyhole into his stable, saw that the light came from a beautiful golden crown placed on the horses' feed-rack, and that it shone without burning. They ran and told the King. On the following night the latter waited for the light to appear, and suddenly entered the stable using his own key. He went off with the crown under his coat, and took it to his bedchamber.

The next day, he called the learned men and magicians of the capital, to tell him the meaning of the inscription on the crown; but none of them could decipher it.

A seven-year-old child, who was there by chance, also saw the crown, and said that it belonged to the Golden-Ram Princess.

The King sent for N'oun-Doaré at once, and spoke to him as follows:

- 'You must bring the Golden-Ram Princess to my court, to be my wife; if you don't, there will only be death for you.'

Poor N'oun-Doaré was all perplexed. He went to his old mare, with tears in his eyes.

- 'I know what's upset you and made you sad,' said the old mare. 'Don't you remember that I told you to leave the crown where you found it, otherwise you would regret it one day? Now that day has come. However, don't despair, for, if you obey me and do everything exactly as I tell you, you can still get out of this spot of trouble. First, go and see the King, and ask him for oats and money for the journey.'

The King gave him oats and money, and N'oun-Doaré set out with his old mare.

They came to the seaside, and saw a little fish stranded on the sand and close to dying.

- 'Put this fish back in the water, quickly,' said the mare.

N'oun-Doaré obeyed, and straight away the little fish lifted its head out of the water, and said:

- 'You've saved my life, N'oun-Doaré; I'm the King of the Fish, and if you ever need my help, you'll only have to call me by the seaside, and I'll come at once.'

And it dived in the water and disappeared.

A little further on, they came across a bird which had been taken in a snare.

- 'Release this bird,' said the mare again.

And N'oun-Doaré released the little bird, which also spoke before flying off:

- 'Thank you, N'oun-Doaré, I'll return you this favour; I'm the King of the Birds, and if ever I or mine can be of service to you, you'll only have to call, and I'll come at once.'

They continued on their way, and, as the mare easily crossed the rivers, mountains, forests, and sea, they soon reached the walls of the Golden-Ram Castle. They heard a great clamour coming from within the castle, so terrifying that N'oun-Doaré dare not go in. Near the door he saw a man chained to a tree, who had as many horns on his body as days in the year.

- 'Unchain this man and set him free,' said the mare.
- 'I daren't go near him.'
- 'Don't be afraid, he won't harm you.'

N'oun-Doaré unchained the man, who said to him:

- 'Thank you, I'll return you this favour; if ever you need help, call for Griffescornu, the Demon King, and I'll come straight away.'

- 'Now go into the castle,' said the mare to N'oun-Doaré,'and fear nothing; I'll stay at pasture here in the woods, where you'll find me when you come back. The mistress of the castle, the Golden-Ram Princess, will welcome you and show you all kinds of wonderful things. You should invite her to come back to the woods with you, to see your mare, which has no equal in the world, and which knows all the dances of Lower Brittany and other lands, which you'll make it perform right under her very eyes.'

N'oun-Doaré set off towards the castle door. He met a servant who was getting water from the spring in the woods, and who asked him what he was doing there.

- 'I wish to speak with the Golden-Ram Princess,' he replied.

The servant went and told her mistress that a stranger had just arrived at the castle, and had asked to speak with her.

The Princess came straight down from her bedchamber, and invited N'oun-Doaré to let her show him all the wonders of the castle.

When he had seen everything, it was his turn to invite the Princess to come to the woods and see his mare. She agreed to this without protest. The mare performed the most varied dances for her, which pleased her very much.

- 'Climb on her back, Princess,' said N'oun-Doaré, 'and she will happily dance with you.'

After some hesitation, the Princess mounted the mare; N'oun-Doaré quickly jumped up behind her, and the mare rose up into the air and transported them, in an instant, over and beyond the sea.

- 'You've tricked me!' exclaimed the Princess; 'but you're not yet at the end of your trials, and you'll weep more than once before I wed the old King of France.'

They went straight to Paris. As soon as they were there, N'oun-Doaré took the Princess and presented her to the King, saying:

- 'Sire, here's the Golden-Ram Princess.'

The King was overwhelmed by her beauty; he could not contain his happiness and wanted to marry her there and then. But the Princess asked them first to bring her ring, which she had left in her bedchamber in the Golden-Ram Castle.

Once more the King charged N'oun-Doaré with the task of fetching the ring.

Sadly, he went back to his mare.

- 'Don't you remember,' said the latter to him, 'that you saved the life of the King of the Birds, and that he promised to return

the favour when an occasion arose?'
- 'I remember,' he replied.
- 'Well now's the time to call for his aid.'
And N'oun-Doaré cried out:
- 'King of the Birds, come and help me, please!'
The King of the Birds came straight away, and said:
- 'What can I do to help you, N'oun-Doaré?'
- 'The King,' he said, 'commands me under pain of death to fetch him the ring which the Golden-Ram Princess left locked in a cabinet in her castle, and for which she has lost the key.'
- 'Don't worry, the ring will be brought to you,' said the bird.
And right away he called every known bird, each by its own name.

They came as each of their names were called; but alas, not one of them was small enough to pass through the keyhole. Only the wren had any chance of doing so, and therefore he was sent to fetch the ring.

With much difficulty and the loss of most of his feathers, he managed to get into the cabinet, take the ring, and bring it to Paris.

N'oun-Doaré ran and gave it to the Princess.
- 'Now Princess,' said the King, 'surely you've no further need to delay my happiness?'
- 'I only need one more thing before I can satisfy you, sire, but I need it, or there will be no wedding,' she replied.
- 'Speak, Princess; what you ask will be done.'
- 'Then have my castle brought here, facing yours.'
- 'Bring your castle here!.... How can you expect such a thing?'
- 'I must have my castle, I tell you, or there will be no wedding.'
And once more N'oun-Doaré was told to find a way of transporting the castle, and he set out with his mare.

When they arrived beneath the walls of the castle, the mare spoke as follows:
- 'Ask the Demon King to help you, the one you released from his chains the first time you were here.'
He called the Demon King, who came and asked:
- 'What can I do to help you, N'oun-Doaré?'
- 'Transport the Golden-Ram Castle to Paris, facing the King's, and right away.'
- 'That's no problem, we'll do it in an instant.'
And the Demon King called his subjects. A whole army of them came and they uprooted the castle from the rock on which it stood, took it up in the air and transported it to Paris. N'oun-

Doaré and his mare followed them, arriving at the same time.

In the morning, the Parisians were quite astonished to see the sun rising on the castle's golden domes, and, thinking there was a fire, they cried out from all sides: 'Fire!....Fire!....' But the Princess easily recognised her castle, and hastened to go there.

- 'Now Princess,' said the King, 'it only remains for you to fix the wedding-day.'

- 'Yes, but I need one thing first,' she replied.

- 'What is it, Princess.'

- 'The key to my castle; they haven't brought it to me, and I can't get in without it.'

- 'I have good locksmiths; they'll make you a new one.'

- 'No! No one in the world can make a key to open my castle door; I must have the old one, from the bottom of the sea.'

On her way to Paris, she had dropped it in the sea.

Again N'oun-Doaré was told to bring the Princess the key to her castle, and he set off with his old mare. When they reached the sea, he called the King of the Fish, who came and said:

- 'What can I do for you, N'oun-Doaré?'

- 'I need the key to the Golden-Ram Castle, which the Princess has thrown into the sea.'

- 'You shall have it,' replied the King.

And at once he called all the fish, who rushed there as he called their names; but none of them had seen the key to the castle. One alone had not responded to the call. He eventually turned up with the key, a priceless diamond, in his mouth. The King of the Fish took it, and gave it to N'oun-Doaré.

N'oun-Doaré and his mare went straight back to Paris, happy and carefree this time, for they knew it was their last trial.

The Princess could no longer play for time, and the day was fixed. They went to Church with great pomp and ceremony, and N'oun-Doaré and his mare followed the procession and, to everyone's astonishment and scandal, went into the Church. But, when the ceremony ended, the mare's skin fell off revealing a most beautiful Princess, who offered her hand to N'oun-Doaré, saying:

- 'I'm the daughter of the King of Tartary; come back to my country, and marry me, N'oun-Doaré.'

And, leaving King and society dumbfounded, they left and I've never heard of them since.

(Told by Vincent Coat, tobacco-factory worker, Morlaix, 1874).

Chapter 4. Princess Blondine*.

Listen, and you will hear;
Believe, if you wish,
Don't believe, if you don't wish to;
Better to believe than go and see.

Once there was a rich Lord who had three sons.

The eldest was called Cado, the second, Méliau, and the third, Yvon.

One day when they were all hunting together in the woods, they met a little old woman, a stranger, who was carrying a jug of water on her head, which she had filled at the spring.

- 'Could you break the jug with an arrow, without touching this little old woman?' Cado asked his brothers.

- 'We wouldn't want to try,' replied Méliau and Yvon, 'from fear of hurting the good woman.'

- 'Well I'm going to do it; just you wait and see.'

And he drew his bow and aimed. He let fly the arrow and it broke the vase. The water drenched the little old woman, who became angry and said to the skilful bowman:

- 'You've done wrong, Cado, and I'll pay you back! From this very moment, all your limbs will tremble just like leaves in the north wind, and it will last until you find Princess Blondine.'

And, at that instant, Cado was taken by a general trembling.

The three brothers went back home and told their father what had happened.

- 'Alas, poor boy, you've done wrong,' said the old gentleman to his eldest son. 'Now you must travel until you find Princess Blondine, like the fairy said, for this little old woman was a fairy. She's the only one in the world who can cure you. I don't know which country she lives in, but I'll give you a letter for my brother, the hermit, who lives in the middle of a forest more than twenty leagues away. Perhaps he'll be able to give you some useful information.'

Cado took the letter and set off.

He walked and he walked, and, by dint of putting one foot in front of the other, he reached his uncle's hermitage. The old man was kneeling in prayer on the threshold of his hut, built in the corner of two rocks, with his hands and eyes lifted up to heaven and as though carried away in ecstasy. Cado waited until

*In Breton, Princis Velandinenn.

he had finished, and then went towards him and said:
- 'Hello, Uncle Hermit.'
- 'You say I'm your uncle, my boy?'
- 'Read this letter, and you'll see that I am, and know why I've come to see you.'

The hermit took the letter, read it, and then he said:
- 'It's true, you really are my nephew. But alas, poor boy, you are far from the end of your travels and sufferings. I'm going to consult my books, to see what I can do for you. You can nibble on this crust of bread whilst you're waiting; it's been my only food for twenty years - I nibble on it whenever I'm hungry, and yet it never gets smaller.'

And Cado set to nibbling the old crust, which was as hard as rock, whilst the hermit consulted his books. But although he searched through them all night, he found no reference to Princess Blondine. The following morning, he said to his nephew:
- 'Here's a letter for a brother-hermit of mine, in another forest twenty leagues away. He has power over all the birds, and perhaps he can give you some useful indication, for neither my science nor my books can tell me anything about Princess Blondine. Here's an ivory ball which will roll itself before you; you only have to follow it, and it will lead you to the door of my brother's hermitage.'

Cado took the letter and the ivory ball. He put the latter on the ground and it rolled itself before him. He followed it. By sunset he was at the door of the rush-and-bough hut of the second hermit.
- 'Hello uncle,' he said as he went up to him.
- 'Your uncle?' replied the old man.
- 'Yes; read this letter and you'll know I am, and why I've come to see you.'

The hermit took the letter, read it, and then said:
- 'Yes, it's true, you really are my nephew. And you're looking for Princess Blondine?'
- 'Yes, uncle; look what a mess I'm in! And my father said that only Princess Blondine could cure me. But neither my father nor my other hermit uncle have been able to tell me where I can find her.'
- 'Nor me, poor boy; I can't say either. But God has made me master of the birds; I'll blow on this silver whistle of mine, and you'll see them come from all sides, big and small; maybe one of them will be able to tell us something about Princess Blondine.'

Princess Blondine.

The old man blew on his silver whistle, and at once clouds of birds of all sizes and colours came over the forest, uttering all sorts of cries. The air was darkened by them. The hermit called them all by their names, one after the other, and asked them if they had seen Princess Blondine during their travels. Not one of them had ever seen her, nor even heard of her.

All the birds had answered the call, except the eagle.

- 'Where can that eagle be?' said the hermit. And he blew harder on his whistle. Then the eagle arrived, in a bad temper, and said:

- 'Why have you made me come here, to die of starvation, when I was doing so well where I was?'

- 'Where were you then?'

- 'I was at Princess Blondine's castle, where I lacked nothing, for there's feasting there every day.'

- 'This is wonderful news, and you're free to go back there, but on condition of carrying my nephew on your back.'

- 'I'll do that happily, if I can have as much to eat as I want.'

- 'Don't worry about that; you'll have as much as you want, glutton that you are.'

Then the hermit went to see the Lord of a neighbouring castle . and begged him to kill one of his best cattle, and bring it, cut in pieces, to his hut. The Lord hastened to give orders to please the hermit, and the beef was brought, already cut up, to his hut. They loaded the meat on the eagle's back. Cado sat on top, and then they went flying above the trees, flap! flap! flap!

Whilst flying through the air, the bird gave Cado the following instructions:

- 'When we're getting close to the castle, which is on an island in the middle of the sea, you'll see a fountain by the shore. Above this fountain there's a beautiful tree with over-hanging branches. Every day at noon, the Princess goes there with her chamber-maid to rest in the shade and comb her fair hair whilst looking at her reflection in the water. You can go towards her without fear. As soon as she sees you, she'll recognise you and make you welcome. She'll give you a pot of ointment to rub over yourself, which will quickly cure you. Then you'll be able to offer to take her away and marry her, in recompense for what she's done for you. She'll accept. Then you should call me, the two of you should climb on my back, and we'll leave right away. Her father's a magician and he'll try to follow us; but he'll be too late.'

The eagle, exhausted by the long journey, often asked for

food.

- 'Give me some food, for I'm weakening,' and Cado gave him some beef, and they went on. They flew over the sea for a long time, seeing only the sky and the water. At last they reached the island. The eagle landed on a rock by the shore. Cado got down, and, having taken a few steps, saw a beautiful tree whose branches reached over a fountain. He could see no one beneath the tree, but it was not yet midday. He hid behind a bush and soon saw a Princess arrive. She was as beautiful as the day, with long fair hair which fell down to her heels, like a cloak. She was accompanied by a waiting-maid who was also very beautiful. They went towards the tree, and the Princess started to comb her beautiful hair whilst looking at her reflection in the water. Then Cado came out from behind his bush; he went to the edge of the water, and the Princess, having seen his reflection there, turned towards him and exclaimed:

- 'Ah! Poor Cado, is it really you? What a state that wicked fairy's put you in! But be brave, poor friend, I'll give you back your health, in spite of her.'

The Princess and her maid set to picking herbs and flowers around the water; then they made an ointment which they gave to Cado, saying:

- 'Rub this ointment over your limbs, and, after twenty-four hours, you'll be cured; then we'll see what to do next.'

- 'Ah! If you cure me of this terrible illness, Princess, I'll show you my gratitude by taking you away from here, if you'll consent to follow me, and I'll marry you.'

- 'I couldn't ask for better, for I'd very much like to leave this island and see the world.'

Cado took the ointment, rubbed it over his body several times, and after twenty-four hours he was completely cured; his limbs no longer trembled.

Then the Princess said to him:

- 'Tomorrow we'll leave promptly at noon, whilst my father's asleep; he has a snooze at noon every day. All three of us will climb on the eagle, for my maid will come with us also. When my father wakes up, he'll know of my flight at once. Then he'll go to his stable, climb on his dromedary, which is faster than the wind, and set out in pursuit. But we'll be well ahead of him, and he won't be able to catch up with us. Stay here, under the tree, until tomorrow. We two are going to spend the night back at the castle. We'll also have one of the cattle killed and cut up, as food for the eagle.'

38

Princess Blondine.

The Princess and her maid went back to the castle, and Cado spent the night by the spring under the tree.

The next day, precisely at noon, the two ladies came back to him. He called his eagle, which came at once. First they loaded the beef on its back, then all three of them climbed on top, and the bird rose laboriously up in the air, for it was heavily loaded.

When the old magician woke up, he called his daughter as usual; but call her as he would, there was no reply. He got up in anger and consulted his books, which told him that the Princess and her maid had left the castle with an adventurer. He ran to his stable, climbed on his dromedary, which did seven leagues an hour, and set out in pursuit.

The overloaded eagle began to weaken, and it slowed down. The Princess was worried, and often looked behind to see if her father was coming. She saw him approaching in a great rage, and, as the eagle was just then passing over a river, she said:

- 'I'm going to drop a little of my ointment in the river, and it will immediately overflow its banks like the sea, and my father won't be able to go any further.'

She threw a little of her ointment into the river, and straight away it swelled up like milk over the fire; it overflowed far and wide, and the old magician was unable to go any further. He was foaming with rage, but what could he do? He set himself to drinking the water, in the hope of drying out the river bed. He drank so much that he died of it.

However the eagle had used up all its stock of meat, and it weakened and threatened to throw off Cado and his two companions.

- 'Give me something to eat,' it cried to Cado.
- 'There's nothing left, poor bird,' replied the latter; 'have courage, for we're getting nearer.'
- 'Give me something to eat, or else I'll let you fall to the ground.'

And Cado cut off one of his buttocks, and gave it to the eagle.

- 'That's good, but it's not very much,' it said.

And a moment later, it said again:

- 'Give me food, I can't last any longer.'
- 'I've nothing more, poor bird. Have courage! Just a few more wing-flaps, and we'll be there.'
- 'Give me food, I tell you, or I'll throw you down.'

And Cado cut off his other buttock, and gave it to the eagle.

Then he cut both his calves off, one after the other, and gave them to it also.

At last they reached the hermit's hut. It was just in time, for the poor eagle was just about finished, and Cado himself was weak, so weak that he seemed on the point of death. But as soon as they were on the ground, the Princess rubbed him with herbs which she collected in the wood where they landed, and immediately his bottom, his calves, and his strength came back. All three of them spent the night in the hermit's hut, sharing his frugal meal, sleeping on a bed of moss and dried leaves collected in the woods. The next morning they set out, after having said farewell to the old hermit. The latter said that he hoped to see them one day, in Paradise, and he gave Cado a letter for his father.

Next they came to the other hermit's hut, and spent the night with him, and, next morning, as they were leaving, the old man also gave Cado a letter for his father.

Cado was now nearing his father's castle, with his two young companions. When they were passing by a wood, the Princess gave him a ring which she had on her finger, and said:

- 'Here's a diamond ring that you must wear on your finger and never give to anyone, otherwise you'll lose your memory of me, and be as though you had never seen me. I'm going to build a castle here, and I'll stay here with my maid until the time comes for us to marry. Then you should come here for me, with your father.'

Cado took the ring, put it on his finger, and promised never to give it to anyone. Then, being unable to persuade the Princess to go with him, despite repeated requests, he went on alone towards his father's castle. When he got there, everyone was happy to see him back, completely cured.

- 'And you haven't brought Princess Blondine with you?' asked his father.

- 'She's staying in a wood, some way from here, and she said she wouldn't come to your castle until you and I go there to fetch her in a fine carriage.'

Straight away the old Lord ordered them to harness his two best horses to his finest carriage, to go and fetch Princess Blondine.

However Cado's sister said to him: - 'Let's walk a little in the garden, brother, to see the beautiful things that have been put there since you left. They'll call us when the carriage is ready.'

Cado went with his sister to see the garden. Whilst he was picking a flower, she noticed the diamond on his finger, straight away desired to possess it, and thought up a plan to take it from her brother. She enticed him to a spring, and they both sat down on the grass, amongst the flowers. Cado was tired, and he rested his head on his sister's knees and quickly went asleep. The young girl took advantage of this, taking his ring and slipping it on her own finger.

A moment later, Cado's father arrived to tell him the carriage was ready.

- 'Eh?' said Cado, rubbing his eyes.
- 'Let's go, without delay.'
- 'Go?.... Go where?'
- 'But you know very well where; to go and fetch Princess Blondine.'
- 'Princess Blondine?.... Who's Princess Blondine?'
- 'Are you asleep? Pull yourself together and let's go at once, for the Princess will grow impatient waiting for us.'
- 'But what Princess, father?'
- 'Let's go, don't pretend you don't know, and let's go quickly and fetch Princess Blondine.'
- 'I don't know what you're talking about, father; I don't know any Princess Blondine.'

And as he seemed to be speaking seriously and sincerely, his father exclaimed sadly: - 'Alas! My poor boy's gone out of his mind! He's suffered so much during his travels! Ah, how unhappy I am!'

And they unharnessed the carriage.

However Cado showed no sign of madness and seemed in full possession of his faculties; it was only when they spoke about his travels and Princess Blondine that he understood nothing; and yet he had a vague souvenir of it all, like a dream that one tries to recall but which stays wrapped in clouds and mist.

The three brothers went hunting in the woods, as before, and Cado was always the best shot and he took as much game himself as his two brothers did together. One day they went further than usual into the woods, and found themselves in front of the castle Princess Blondine had built by magic; for she also was a magician. They were astonished to see so beautiful a castle, and they looked at it for a long time, in silence.

- 'What a beautiful castle!' they said; 'but how did it get there? We've been here many times, and we've never seen anything like it until today. Who do you think lives in it? Some

41

magician perhaps?'

At last, after having looked at the wonderful castle for a long time, they decided to try to gain entry, under pretext of asking for a drink of milk or cider, or asking the way as people do when they are lost. They knocked on the door and it opened at once. The Princess herself came to greet them in the courtyard, and she invited them into her palace, honouring them in a friendly way. Cado did not recognise her; she recognised him as soon as she saw him, but did not let it show. The three brothers were charmed by her beauty and friendliness. She invited them to dine with her and to spend the night in her castle, which they could not refuse. Dinner was a happy event, for the three hunters found the wine, and their hostess, excellent. Mēliau could not keep his eyes off the Princess, and he said softly to Cado, who was next to him:

- 'I fancy our hostess very much.'
- 'See if you can make love to her,' replied Cado.

After the meal, Mēliau told the Princess how he felt about her, and she seemed so pleased to hear this, that she said: - 'I'll give you a room next to mine, and, when your brothers are asleep, you can come quietly to me.'

Mēliau was overjoyed. At midnight, when everyone else was asleep, he got up and gently knocked on Princess Blondine's door. She opened it and received him in a very friendly way. She gave him a fresh shirt, which she asked him to put on before getting into bed. Mēliau hurried to change his shirt; but, when he was putting on the one the Princess had given him, he felt it becoming hard and cold as ice, and all night he stayed put with his arms stuck out and his shirt half on, without being able to take it off nor put it on properly. He begged hard for the Princess to help him, but she did not reply and left him crying. He remained in this fix all night. When the sun rose, his shirt became supple; then he could rid himself of it, and he fled and ran straight back to his brothers.

- 'Well, did you enjoy the night?' Cado asked him.

He told them his adventure in all its details, and the other two laughed, as well you might believe.

Then the three brothers said to themselves: - 'We're with a magician here, and we'd best move off as quickly as we can.' And they left without saying goodbye to their hostess.

When they reached the house, their father, who was worried because they had not come back at night, as they usually did, asked them:

- 'Where did you spend the night?'

And they told their father everything, and added:

- 'There's a fine castle there, father, and a beautiful Princess!'

The old man thought that this might well be Princess Blondine's castle, and he promised himself that he would look into it, but he said nothing to his children.

Meanwhile, Cado wished to marry a Princess he had loved before his travels. His proposal was accepted, his father gave his consent, and the wedding-day was fixed. They invited everyone in the land, rich and poor, to take part in the festivities which would take place. Yvon said to his father:

- 'I think it would be a good thing to invite the Princess who so graciously received us in her palace.'

- 'You're right, my boy,' he replied, 'I'll go myself to invite her, and you can come with me.'

One fine morning, the old man and his youngest son set out in a superb carriage to invite the mistress of the castle in the forest. They reached the wonderful castle and were received in the best manner possible. The old man was amazed and dumbfounded when he saw the Princess, so beautiful did he find her. At last, when he could speak, he said to her: - 'I have come, incomparable Princess, to beg you to do me the honour of taking part in my eldest son's wedding celebrations. He is marrying Princess Brunette in eight days' time.'

- 'I accept with great pleasure,' replied the Princess, 'and I'll be there on the appointed day.'

- 'I'll send my carriage for you,' replied the father.

- 'Don't go to such trouble, my Lord, for I also have a carriage, as you shall see.'

The old man could not take his eyes away from the Princess, for he was overwhelmed by her beauty. Yvon was also lost in admiration, and he did not speak a word. They both returned home in silence, dreaming about her.

At last the wedding-day came. All the guests had already arrived, in their best festive clothing, except for the mistress of the castle in the woods. Cado became impatient, and did not wish to wait any longer; but his father said they should not go to the Church until the unknown Princess arrived. At last, she arrived also, in a gilded carriage, so shining that they could not look at it, and drawn by four horses which made the others there look like old nags. She was all covered in gold, silk and diamonds, and her fair hair, shining like gold, reached the ground behind her. All the women there, seeing themselves eclipsed by her, raged with spite. The bridegroom's sister, who had her brother's diamong ring on her finger, was all proud and conceited.

They went to Church with great pomp, and even the sun paled before Princess Blondine. They were all taken up by her, and the young bride-to-be, beautiful and gracious also, was greatly vexed.

On returning from the Church, they sat down to a magnificent feast. One of the guests, pushed by his wife, ventured to speak to the unknown one, and said:

- 'Clearly you're not from these parts, beautiful Princess.'
- 'No,' she replied, 'I come from far away.'
- 'And are you married?'
- 'No, I'm not married; I was engaged, but he broke his word.'

Cado was sitting close to her, and, noticing the fine diamond on her finger, he said:

- 'What a magnificent diamond you have, Princess.'
- 'Yes,' she replied, 'it's a fine diamond;' and, pulling the ring off her finger, she gave it to the new husband, saying:
- 'Try it; I think it will suit you perfectly.'

Cado took the ring, put it on his finger, and at once, as if he had awakened from a long sleep, he recognised the Princess and remembered all that had happened.

- 'Hello!' he exclaimed; 'now I've two wives instead of one; but the first is always the best and dearest to my heart.'

And he gave her his hand, to the great astonishment of all the guests, and they went back to Church where Cado was married for a second time in the same day. As for Princess Brunette, his brother Méliau married her also, so as not to leave her without a husband on her wedding-day.

Yvon also fell in love with Princess Blondine's maid, so they had three weddings at the same time.

And there was feasting and dancing for a whole month. I myself was young at the time, and had to pluck the partridges, chickens and ducks, and never in my life have I seen, nor will I ever see, such feasting.

(Told by Ann Drann, maid-servant, Plouguernevel, 1855).

Chapter 5. The Princess of the Shining Star.

Once, near Léguer, there was a miller who went out one day with his gun, to hunt swans and ducks on the millpond.

It was December, and the ground was covered in snow.

When he came to the water's edge, he noticed a duck splashing about in the water. He aimed and fired; as soon as he did so, he was quite surprised to find a beautiful Princess standing next to him, who had come from he-didn't-know-where, and who spoke to him as follows:

- 'Thank you, kind sir! I've been kept here for a long time, enchanted in the form of a duck, by three demons who never give me any peace. You've brought me back my human form, and, with a little courage and perseverence, you can completely deliver me from their clutches.'

- 'What must I do for that?' asked the astonished miller.

- 'Spend three nights in succession in the old ruined manor you can see up there.'

- 'And what's there? The devil perhaps?'

- 'Alas! There's not only one devil, but twelve devils that will torment you. They'll throw you several times from one end of the great hall to the other, and they'll even throw you in the fire. Don't be afraid, whatever happens to you, and have faith in me, for I've an ointment which will keep you alive and cure you, even if all your limbs are broken and crushed. Even if you were killed, I could resuscitate you. If you can endure these three nights for me, without complaining nor speaking a single word, you'll not regret it later. Beneath the hearthstone of the old manor there are three casks of gold and three of silver; they will all be yours, and myself also in the bargain, if you wish. Are you man enough to face the task?'

- 'Even if there were a hundred devils, instead of twelve, I'd face up to it,' replied the miller.

And then the Princess disappeared, and he went back to his mill, thinking about what he was going to see and hear.

Night came and he went to the old manor with firewood to make a fire and cider and tobacco so he could drink and smoke whilst keeping warm.

Towards midnight he heard a great clamour coming from the chimney, and, although he was not nervous, he hid under an old bed from where he saw eleven devils come down the chimney.

They were surprised to find a fire burning in the hearth.

- 'What's going on?' they asked one another.

- 'Where's the Lame Devil?' - 'He's always late,' said another devil, who seemed to be their chief.

- 'Here he comes,' said a third.

And the Lame Devil came by the same route as the others, and asked:

- 'What's new here, comrades?'

- 'Nothing,' they replied.

- 'Nothing?... Well, as for me, I claim that the miller of Léguer Bridge is here, somewhere, and that he's come to try to take the Princess away from us. Let's look for him.'

And they looked everywhere. The Lame Devil looked under the bed and, seeing the cowering miller, exclaimed:

- 'Here he is, under the bed!'

And he dragged him out by one of his feet.

- 'Ah miller, nice miller!' he said laughing derisively, 'you want to take the Princess away? You like pretty girls, do you?'

- 'First of all, my friend, we're going to play a game which won't be quite to your liking, but which will cure you of the idea of wanting to take the Princess away from us.'

And they threw him again and again, like a ball, from one end of the hall to the other; and yet the poor miller did not speak a word. Seeing this, they threw him through the window into the courtyard, and, as he neither made a sound nor moved, they believed him dead.

Then the cock crowed, announcing the day, and they went at once by the way they had come, that's to say by the chimney.

Then the Princess came with a pot of ointment in her hand, and she rubbed it over the miller, who got up and found himself as fit and well as ever.

- 'You've suffered a great deal, my friend,' said the Princess.

- 'Yes Princess, I've suffered a lot,' he replied.

- 'You still have to spend two such nights to deliver me from these wicked devils.'

- 'From what I've seen, it's no laughing matter delivering a Princess, but I'll stick it out to the end.'

Night came and he went a second time to the old manor, where he hid himself under a pile of wood at the end of the hall. The twelve devils came down the chimney at midnight, just like the night before.

- 'I smell a Christian!' said the Lame Devil.

And they sought and found the miller again, in the wood-pile.

- 'Ah! It's you again, miller! Why aren't you dead after last night's game? But don't worry, we'll be finished with you this time, and it won't take long.'

And they threw him into a cauldron full of oil, and brought it to the boil over the fire.

The cock crowed to announce the dawn, and the devils left again.

The Princess came at once and pulled the miller out of the cauldron. He was cooked, and his flesh was falling off the bone; yet she resuscitated him again, with her ointment.

The third night the devils were once more astonished at finding the miller still alive:

- 'This is the last night; if we don't finish him this time, we'll lose everything. He must be protected by some magician. What should we do?'

Each one gave his opinion, and the Lame Devil said:

- 'We should make a good fire, roast him on a skewer, and then eat him.'

- 'That's it!' said the others, 'let's roast him and eat him.'

But their deliberations and preparations had taken up too much time, and just when they were about to skewer the miller and put him over the fire, the cock crowed and they had to leave the scene; they knocked down the gable of the house as they left, making a terrible din.

The Princess came once more with her ointment, but she did not need it this time. She embraced the miller in her great joy, and said:

- 'It's all going well! You've delivered me and now the treasure belongs to you.'

And they pushed the hearthstone to one side, and found three casks of gold, and three of silver.

- 'Take the gold and silver,' said the Princess, 'and use it as you wish. As for me, I can't yet stay with you; first I must undertake a journey which will last a year and a day, after which we'll always be together.'

And then the Princess disappeared. The miller regretted it somewhat, but he easily consoled himself by thinking of his treasure. He handed his mill over to his manservant and set out on his travels with a friend, whilst waiting for the return of the Princess. They visited far-off lands, and, as they were not short of money, they did not deny themselves any pleasure.

After eight months of this life, the miller said to his friend:

- 'Let's go back now, to our country, for we're a long way off and I don't want to miss the *rendez-vous* with the Princess, at the end of a year and a day.'

And they set off home. On the way they met an old woman by the roadside, who had some fine-looking apples in a basket; and the old woman said to them:

- 'Buy my apples, good sirs.'

- 'Don't buy any apples from that old woman,' said the miller's friend to him.

- 'Why not?' replied the miller, 'I'll eat an apple with pleasure.'

And he bought three apples and ate one of them right away, and felt poorly.

When the day came when the Princess should arrive, he went to the agreed spot in the woods, accompanied by his friend. Whilst they were waiting, for they had arrived early, he ate another of the apples he had bought from the old woman, and at once he felt sleepy. He sat down on the grass at the foot of a tree, and fell asleep.

Soon after, the Princess arrived in a beautiful star-coloured carriage drawn by ten horses, which were also star-coloured. When she saw that the miller was asleep, she became sad and asked his friend why he had fallen asleep.

- 'I don't rightly know,' he replied, 'but he bought some apples from an old woman we met by the roadside; he's just eaten one of them, and at once he became sleepy.'

- 'Alas! It must be that, for the old woman from whom he bought the apples is a witch who only wishes us evil. I can't take him with me in that state, but I'll come back twice more, tomorrow and the day after, and if I find him awake, I'll take him in my carriage. Here's a golden pear and a handkerchief you can give him when he awakes, and you can tell him I'll come back at the same time tomorrow.'

And then the Princess rose up in the air, in her star-coloured carriage, and disappeared.

The miller awoke a moment later, and his friend told him what had happened whilst he was asleep. He gave him the pear and the handkerchief, and told him that the Princess would be back tomorrow, and then again the day after, if he was still asleep.

He was upset and said:

- 'I won't be asleep tomorrow.'

And he went to bed as soon as he got back home, so as not to be sleepy the next day.

On the following day he went back to the wood with his friend; but he became absent-minded and ate the witch's third apple, which he found in his pocket, and he fell asleep again.

This time the Princess came in a moon-coloured carriage, and

on seeing him again, she exclaimed:
- 'Alas! He's asleep again!'

Then she said to his friend:
- 'I'll come back tomorrow, but it will be for the last time. Here's another golden pear and a handkerchief for you to give him when he wakes up, and you can tell him that if I find him asleep again tomorrow, he'll never see me again unless he crosses three powers and three seas in his search for me.'

And she rose up in the air, in her moon-coloured carriage, and disappeared.

When the miller woke up, his friend told him how the Princess had left when she found him asleep again, and that she had said that she would come back for the last time tomorrow, and that if she found him asleep, he would never see her again unless he crossed three powers and three seas to find her. Then he gave him the second pear and the second handkerchief.

The poor miller was inconsolable, and he said to his friend:
- 'In God's name, prevent me from sleeping tomorrow; don't stop talking to me, so that I'll stay awake.'

But despite all, when the Princess arrived next day in a sun-coloured carriage*, he was asleep again.
- 'Alas! You're asleep again, poor friend!' she exclaimed sadly, 'and what's more, I can't come back.' - And, addressing his friend, she said: - 'Tell him that, to see me again, he must seek me in the Kingdom of the Shining Star, after crossing three powers and three seas to get there, which he'll not be able to do without great trouble and pain. Here's a third golden pear and a third handkerchief which you can give him, and which will be useful to him later on.'

And she rose up in the air in her carriage, and disappeared.

When the miller woke up and learnt that the Princess had left for good, he began to cry and tear his hair out in desperation. It was sad to see him like that. Then he said:
- 'I'll seek her and find her, even if I have to go through hell!'

And he set out at once on the quest of the Kingdom of the Shining Star. He walked and he walked, further and further, without stopping day or night. He found himself in a great forest, which seemed to have no end. After wandering aimlessly there for several days and nights, he climbed a tree and saw a little

---

*(The storyteller had the sequence of carriage colours star-sun-moon. Luzel thought he had put the sun before the moon by mistake, and the sequence star-moon-sun has therefore been adopted in the text).

light in the distance. He went towards it and found himself in front of a poor hut made of tree branches and hay. He pushed on the door, which was ajar, and saw within an old man with a long white beard.

- 'Good evening, grandfather,' he said to him.
- 'Good evening, young man,' replied the astonished old man; 'seeing you gives me pleasure, for, until now, I've not set eyes on a single human being during the eighteen hundred years I've been here. You're welcome to come in and tell me something of what's been going on in the world, for it's so long since I had any news.'

The miller went in and told him his name, his country, and the reason for his travels.

- 'I'll do something for you, my boy,' said the old man. 'Here are two enchanted gaiters which were very useful to me when I was your age, but which I no longer need. When you wear them on your legs you can do seven leagues at each step, and you'll be able to reach the Castle of the Shining Star, which is very far from here, without too much trouble.'

The miller spent the night in the old hermit's hut, and next morning at sunrise, he put his gaiters on, and left.

Now he could cover the ground. Nothing stopped him, neither streams, rivers, forests nor mountains. Towards sunset he saw another hut similar to the other one, on the edge of a forest, and, as he was hungry and a little tired, he said to himself:

- 'I must ask for food and lodging at this hut; perhaps they'll also give me some useful advice.'

He pushed his way easily through the broom hedge, and saw a little old woman, with teeth as long as your arm, crouching on the hearthstone, amongst the ashes at the back of the hut.

- 'Good evening, grandmother,' he said; 'would you be so kind as to give me hospitality for the night?'
- 'Alas, my boy,' she replied, 'you've fallen badly here and the best thing you can do is to clear off as quickly as possible. I've three sons who are terrible, and if they find you here, I fear greatly they'll eat you. Clear off, I tell you, for they'll soon be here.'
- 'What are your sons called, grandmother?'
- 'Their names are: January, February and March.'
- 'Then you're the Mother of the Winds?'
- 'Yes, I'm the Mother of the Winds; but clear off, I tell you, for they're coming.'
- 'In God's name, grandmother, give me hospitality and hide me

50

somewhere where they won't find me.'

And right then they heard a great noise outside.

- 'That's January, my eldest son, coming,' said the old woman. 'What can we do?.... I'll tell him you're my nephew, one of my brother's sons, and that you've come to pay me a visit and get to know your cousins. Tell them your name's Yves Pharaon, and be nice to them.'

Straight away an enormous giant rushed down the chimney, with a white beard and hair, shivering with cold, and going 'Brrr! Brrr! Brrr!.... I'm hungry, mother, I'm cold and hungry!.... Brrr!'

- 'Sit yourself there, near the fire, son,' said the old woman to him, 'and I'll prepare your supper.'

But the giant soon saw the miller, crouching in a corner, and asked:

- 'What's this earthworm here, mother? I'll swallow it whilst waiting for my supper....'

- 'Be good and stay on your stool, son, and see that you do no harm to this boy; it's little Yves Pharaon, my nephew and your cousin.'

- 'I'm very hungry, mother, and I want to eat him,' said the giant, showing his teeth.

- 'Stay there quietly, I tell you, and don't do any harm to this boy, or watch out for the sack....'

And she pointed her finger at a large sack hanging from a beam. Then the giant kept still and didn't say another word.

The old woman's two other sons, February and March, arrived also, one after the other, making a terrible din. Trees cracked and fell, stones flew through the air, and the wolves howled. It was terrifying! The old woman had her time cut out protecting her *protégé* from the giants' voracity, and she only managed it by threatening them with the sack.

At last, they all sat down together, like good friends, and in next to no time they had devoured three entire cattle and drunk three casks of wine. When the giants were satisfied, they calmed down and chatted peacefully with their sham cousin. January asked him:

- 'Tell us now, cousin, if your journey hasn't any other reason besides visiting us?'

- 'Yes, dear cousins, I wish to go as far as the Castle of the Shining Star, and if you could show me the way, you'd be doing me a great favour.'

- 'I've never heard tell of the Castle of the Shining Star,' replied January.

- 'I've heard of it all right, but I don't know where it is,' said March.

- 'I know where it is,' said February; 'I even passed by it only yesterday, and I saw them making great preparations for the wedding, for the Princess is getting married tomorrow. They've slaughtered a hundred head of cattle, as well as many calves, sheep, chickens and ducks - I can't say exactly how many - for the great feasts that will take place there.'

- 'The Princess is getting married!' exclaimed the miller; 'I must be there before the ceremony; tell me how to get there, cousin February.'

- 'You couldn't ask me at a better time,' replied February; 'I'm going back there tomorrow, but you won't be able to keep up with me.'

- 'Yes I will. I've gaiters with which I can do seven leagues at each step.'

- 'Good! We can set off together in the morning.'

January set off first, with a great noise, around midnight. February left about an hour later, taking the miller with him. The latter followed him without difficulty until they reached the sea; but there he had to stop.

- 'Help me across the sea, cousin,' he said to February.

- 'There's not just one sea, but three seas we have to cross,' replied February, 'and I fear I'll not be able to carry you so far on my back.'

- 'In God's name, cousin, take me on your back.'

- 'I'll carry you as long as I can, but I warn you that if I become tired, I'll throw you down.'

He climbed on February's back, and off they went over the great sea. They crossed one sea, two seas, but, towards the middle of the third sea, February said:

- 'I'm tired and can't carry you any further; I'm going to drop you in the water.'

- 'In God's name, dear cousin, don't do that; we're getting close; I can see land; one last effort and we'll be there.'

At last February reached the land, after much trouble, and set his burden down outside the walls of the town where the Princess had her castle.

Soon after, March came along, and the miller said to him:

- 'Cousin March, cousin March, listen.'

- 'What do you want, cousin Yves Pharaon?' said March.

- 'February put me down here, at the foot of these high walls

which I can't climb; take me to the other side on your back.'
- 'Willingly - climb on,' said March.

And he climbed on March's back, who set him down on the other side of the wall, in the town, and went on his way.

The miller went to an inn and, after breakfast, entered into conversation with the landlady and asked her:
- 'What's new in town, landlady?'
- 'They only talk of the wedding of the Princess of the Shining Star, which will take place today,' she replied.
- 'Really? Then she's found a husband to suit her?'
- 'They say she's getting married somewhat despite herself, and that she doesn't like the Prince she's going to marry. The procession will soon be going past the front of the inn, on the way to Church.'

The miller put the first pear and handkerchief the Princess had left him, on a small table in front of the inn; then he waited.

The procession came by shortly afterwards, led by the Princess and her *fiancé*. The Princess noticed the pear and the handkerchief and recognised them, as well as the miller, who was waiting close by. She stopped briefly, said she was suddenly unwell and asked them to put the ceremony off until the following day. This was done without anyone suspecting her motive.

The procession went back to the palace, and when the Princess was in her bedchamber, she sent one of her ladies to buy her the pear and handkerchief from the miller.

The lady brought them to her.

Next day, the procession set off again towards the Church, going by the same route. The miller had put a second pear and handkerchief on a table in front of the inn. On seeing them, the Princess pretended to be suddenly indisposed again, and the procession went back, as on the previous day. She sent the same lady to buy this second pear and handkerchief.

Finally, the same thing happened on the third day, except that the Princess told her messenger to bring the miller to her, which she did.

The Princess and the miller embraced tenderly and wept tears of joy at finding one another again.

However her *fiancé*, the Prince, said that, since the Princess was always indisposed on the way to Church, the wedding feast should take place anyway, and they could go to Church later.

And they sat down to a magnificent feast, each one dressed as richly as possible. The Princess was so beautiful that she lit up the hall like the sun. By the end of the meal everyone was happy and talkative, and they took turns at singing and story-telling. The father-in-law said to the Princess:

- 'It's your turn, Princess. Tell us something.'

- 'There's something, father-in-law, which embarrasses me very much, and I would like your advice on it; I have a pretty little casket, which had a nice little golden key, which I liked very much. I lost the key, and had a new one made. But it happens that I've just found the old key before having even tried the new one. The old one was very good, and I don't yet know how good the new one will be. Tell me, please, to which of the two I should give preference, the old or the new one?'

-'You should always regard and respect what is old,' replied the old man; 'I would like, however, to see the two keys before deciding definitely for one or the other.'

- 'Good!' said the Princess; 'I'll show you both of them.'

And she got up from the table, went to her bedchamber, and came back holding the miller by the hand, saying:

- 'Here's the old key, lost and just recovered; as for the new key, it's the young Prince of Céans, to whom I'm well engaged, but, seeing that the religious ceremony has not taken place, I feel free to give my hand where I please. As you have said most clearly, sir, what is old merits respect and consideration. There-fore I'll keep my old key, and I leave you the new one. Now, by the old key I mean this courageous and faithful young man (and she indicated the miller) who, after having delivered me from the castle where an evil magician kept me prisoner, has come here in search of me at the price of a thousand troubles; as for the new key, it's your own son, you understand; I was on the point of marrying him, but I give him his freedom back this very day.'

Great was the amazement of all the company, on hearing these words, as you might well imagine.

The Princess and the miller left at once, without anyone trying to stop them; they went to the courtyard and galloped away in a gilded carriage drawn by four superb horses.

They went to Gueodet in Lower Brittany, where there was then a fine town; they were married in Church and there was feasting and rejoicing such as I've never seen - except perhaps in a dream.

(Told by Allain Richard, fisherman, Gueodet, Lannion, 1874).

Commentary.

The antiquity of these stories is witnessed by their reference to shamanism, or its derivatives, and by the solar symbolism of the Golden-Haired Princess who, in the third story, is said to have 'lit up the hall like the sun.' Although these stories may be taken literally as tales of adventure in another world, their profound interpretation, once again, is of man's inner spiritual quest, symbolised as an outer journey in search of the Princess, and ending in marriage, representing the acquisition of a permanent spiritual state.

N'oun-Doaré begins with the story of a young man with strange tastes. From a spiritual point of view, worldly peoples' senses of value are confused, or even topsy-turvy, so that spiritually-orientated people appear to them to be strange, or even quite crazy. Some may see N'oun-Doaré's mare as a manifestation of the ancient Mare-Goddess, but, within the context of the story, the mare is an enchanted princess - human or fairy - and in other versions of the story the Princess is enchanted in other animal forms. The story of the enchanted Princess may take this tale back to ancient times when there were shamans who were said to be able to take on animal forms, and to do likewise for other people, and forms of witchcraft derived from shamanism said to give the witch similar powers. From a more profound, esoteric point of view, N'oun-Doaré's seeing the Princess first in the form of a mare, may be interpreted as man at the beginning of the spiritual quest having only a vague notion of the nature of the 'spirit within himself.' True knowledge of the inner spiritual nature only comes later, at the end of the quest, symbolised in this story by the Princess casting off her animal skin and revealing herself in her full beauty... Throughout this story there is a strong element of destiny; N'oun-Doaré is obliged to undertake the quest by the King of France, under pain of death. His early meetings with the Fish, Bird, and Demon Kings, who are 'set up' ready for him to rescue them, and who will be obliged to help him later, underline this element of predestination. The quest part of the story, full of wonder and magic, may be interpreted as pure imagination; it also serves, however, to symbolise the 'lesser mysteries' as a crossing of the 'lower waters' - the world of the psyche - a world full of dangers, illusions, and distractions.

In the second story, we have kept Luzel's **Princess Blondine**, rather than translate the title as 'The Blond Princess', not to mention the off-putting alternative of 'Princess Goldilocks.' This story, like the previous one, contains a strong element of destiny, for Cado, after foolishly upsetting a fairy, is inflicted with a general trembling which forces him to undertake the quest of the Princess. Cado's foolish act is caused by his own ego, which is seen therefore as the cause of his troubles; the quest will lead to the death of the ego and a spiritual rebirth, and hence the end of his troubles. The first part of Cado's journey refers back to ancient times when there were sage-hermits in the Celtic forests; the second hermit's command over the birds no doubt refers to shamanism, as also the flight on the eagle's back. In an older version of the story, it is possible that Cado may have been metamorphosed into an eagle. Flight, by one means or another, is, however, a common element in traditional stories the world over; from a more profound point of view, it represents the flight of the soul.

In this story the Princess is shown as being kept prisoner by a wicked magician. From an interior, symbolic point of view, the wicked magician represents man's worldly attachments, distractions, desires, and vices which prevent him from knowing the 'spirit within himself,' keeping it locked up like a prisoner.

Cado's brother's imprisonment in the shirt may be interpreted as a disqualification, perhaps through wrong motivation, and also as implying that there are no short-cuts.

The spiritual quest requires continual orientation and concentration, or 'remembrance,' symbolised by the ring the Princess gave to Cado. Losing the ring represents Cado's falling into 'forgetfulness' of his spiritual way; he almost fails in the quest. His recovery of the ring, representing a return to 'remembrance,' permits him to complete the quest, symbolised by his marriage to the Princess.

This story seems to have suffered from interpolation and modification, and Luzel's storyteller was somewhat lacking in logic. The dromedary was hardly an appropriate pursuit animal for a magician living on an 'island in the middle of the sea;' his arrest by a swollen river also makes little sense in this context. At the end of the story we have to assume that the Princess had at least two rings, for the original one was still being worn by Cado's sister! Despite these logical inconsistences, the story is entertaining and the basic symbolism is retained.

In the **Princess of the Shining Star** we see a fuller, and in many ways more 'authentic' story, allowing for modifications such as the miller hunting with a gun, and the marriage taking *place in Church.*

The Princess, enchanted in the form of a duck, may be interpreted as a reference to the form of witchcraft derived from shamanism. The esoteric interpretation, once again, is that the Princess appears like a duck because man, at the beginning of the quest, has only a vague notion of the 'spirit within himself.' In another version of the story, 'The Sunflower Princess' (Princess Troiol), the Princess appears in the form of a she-goat. The demons who have enchanted and imprisoned the Princess, and those with whom the miller has to contend, represent his worldly attachments, desires, and vices, which have to be overcome. At this stage the miller has only a few brief encounters with the Princess - brief glimpses of the spirit - and he has to wait a year and a day before the possibility of something more permanent... When the day arrives, he is tricked by a witch into eating an apple which makes him fall asleep; equivalent to man letting himself fall into 'forgetfulness.'

The Princess arrives first in a star-coloured, then a moon-coloured, and finally a sun-coloured carriage. The star and moon may be regarded as symbolising 'reflections' of the spirit, in two different degrees; the sun symbolising the spirit. The miller misses his opportunities at these encounters; he is obliged to undertake a formidable quest to the Kingdom of the Shing Star, if he is ever to see the Princess again. He meets a sage-hermit in the forest, who gives him a pair of seven-league gaiters - possibly implying shamanistic means of the soul leaving the body and travelling. Then he comes close to the more terrible aspects of the Divinity, in the form of Wind-Gods. As in an earlier story, he is protected by the Mother-Goddess, and her sons help him to complete his quest. The Princess sees his tokens (pears and handkerchiefs) and they go away to be married.

Near the end of the story the Princess says the miller had delivered her from a castle where a wicked magician had kept her prisoner; at the beginning it was a manor and some demons! This inconsistency neither detracts from the story nor its symbolism. The fact that the Princess is about to marry someone else may be little more than a storyteller's device to keep up the suspense towards the end.

PART 4. THE PSYCHE MYTH.

Chapter 6. The Foal-Man.

Once, in old Kerouez Castle, at Loguivi-Plougras, there was a rich and powerful Lord whose only son had come into the world with a foal's head, much to the distress of his family. When the foal-headed boy was eighteen, he told his mother one day that he wished to get married, and that she should go and ask the farmer for one of his three pretty young daughters.

The good woman went to see the farmer's wife, somewhat embarrassed by her errand. After having chatted for a long time about her cattle, her children and umpteen other things, she at last explained the reason for her visit.

- 'Jesus, madam! What are you saying? Give my daughter, a Christian, to a man with an animal's head?' exclaimed the farmer's wife.

- 'Don't be too put off by that, my poor woman. God gave him to me like that, and he's unhappy enough as it is, poor boy! As for the rest of him, he's sweetness and goodness itself, and your daughter would be happy with him.'

- 'I'll ask my daughters, and if one of them accepts, I'll not oppose her in any way.'

And the good woman went to find her daughters, and explained to them the reason for the Lady of the Castle's visit.

- 'How dare you make us such a proposition?' replied the two elder daughters; 'marry someone with a foal's head! We'd really have to be short of gallants, and, thank God, we're not.'

- 'But think how rich he is, and an only son; the castle and all that goes with it would be yours.'

- 'That's true,' replied the eldest, 'then I'd be the Lady of the Castle! Well, tell him I consent to marry him.'

The mother told the Lady of her eldest daughter's reply, and the latter went happily back to the castle to tell her son the news.

They began preparing for the wedding at once.

A few days later, the young *fiancée* was in the woods near the washing-place, watching the servants washing the linen, chatting and laughing with them. One of them said to her:

- 'How can a pretty girl like you marry someone with a foal's head?'

- 'Bah!' she replied; 'he's rich, and in any case, don't worry, he won't be my husband for long, for I'll cut his throat on my wedding night.'

Just then there came a handsome Lord who, having heard the

conversation, said:

- 'That's a strange conversation you're having there!'
- 'These washer-women, my Lord,' replied the young *fiancée*, 'are mocking me because I've consented to marry the young Lord of the Castle, who has a foal's head; but I won't be that animal's wife for long, for I'll cut his throat on my wedding night.'
- 'You'll do well,' replied the stranger. And he went on his way and disappeared.

At last the wedding-day arrived. There was feasting and re-joicing in the castle. When the time came, the bridesmaids led the young wife to the nuptial chamber, undressed her, put her to bed, and then retired. Then the young husband came along, handsome and shining; for, after sunset he lost his foal's head and became just like other men. He ran to the bed, leant over the young wife as if to embrace her, and then cut her head off!

Next morning, when his mother came, she was horrified at what she saw, and cried out:

- 'God, whatever have you done, son?'
- 'I've done to her what she wished to do to me, mother.'

Three months later, the Lord with the foal's head was taken again by the desire to marry, and he begged his mother to go and ask for the farmer's second daughter. The latter was no doubt ignorant of the way in which her sister had perished; she also eagerly accepted the proposition which was made to her, once more because of the young Lord's worldly goods.

The wedding preparations began at once, and one day when she, like her sister, was laughing and talking with the washer-women from the castle, one of them said to her:

- 'How can a pretty girl like you take a man with a foal's head as a husband? And then, you'd better watch out, for no one knows exactly what happened to your sister.'
- 'Don't worry, I'll soon rid myself of that animal; I'll kill him like a pig, on my wedding night, and all his goods will belong to me.'

Just then the same unknown Lord came by; he stopped for a moment and said:

- 'That's a strange conversation you're having, girls!'
- 'These girls, my Lord, are trying to dissuade me from marry-ing the young Master of the Castle, because he has a foal's head; but I'll slaughter him like a pig on my wedding night, and all his goods will belong to me.'
- 'You'll do well,' replied the unknown one - and he disappeared.

The wedding was celebrated with solemnity, and, as on the first occasion, there were magnificent feasts, music, dances, and all kinds of games; but next morning the young bride was again found in bed with her head cut off!....

Three months later, the young Lord with the foal's head asked his mother to go and ask for the farmer's third daughter. The parents objected this time; the lot of their two elder daughters made them afraid; but an offer to cede them the farm in its entirety proved irresistible. Moreover the young girl herself consented, and said to her mother:

- 'I'll take him willingly, mother; if my two sisters lost their lives, it was their own fault; their tongue was the cause of it.'

They made wedding preparations at the castle for the third time. Just like her two sisters, the young *fiancée* went to chat with the washer-women:

- 'How can a pretty girl like you,' they said, 'marry someone with a foal's head, especially after what happened to your two elder sisters?'

- 'Yes, yes,' she replied with assurance; 'I'll marry him and I've no fear of the same thing happening to me; if something bad happened to them, it was their tongue which caused it.'

Just then the same Lord came by and heard the conversation; this time he went on his way without saying anything.

The wedding took place with great pomp and ceremony. There were magnificent feasts, music, dances and games and entertainments of all kinds, as on the two previous occasions. The only difference was that, on the next morning, the young bride was still alive. She lived happily for nine months with her husband. The latter only had his foal's head during the day; after sunset he became a handsome young man until the morning.

After nine months the young wife gave birth to a son, a fine child, well-conformed and without a foal's head. When he was about to take the child to be baptised, the father said to his young wife:

- 'I've been condemned to bear a foal's head until a child was born to me; now I'm about to be delivered, and, as soon as my son is baptised, I'll be just like other men; but say nothing whatsoever of this until the baptismal bells have stopped ringing; if you say the least word of it, even to your mother, I shall instantly disappear, and you'll never see me again.'

Having given this advice, he left with the Godfather and Godmother to have his son baptised.

Soon the young mother heard the sound of the bells from her

bed, and she was full of happiness. In her impatience to tell the good news to her mother, who was close to her bed, she could not wait for them to stop ringing, and spoke. Straight away she saw her husband arrive with his foal's head, covered in dust and very angry.

- 'Ah, what misfortune!' he cried. 'What have you done? Now I must leave, and you'll never see me again.'

And he left at once, without even embracing her.

She got up to hold him back; being unable to do so, she ran after him.

- 'Don't follow me,' he cried out to her.

But she did not listen, and kept on running.

- 'I tell you, don't follow me.'

She was on his heels and about to catch up with him; then he turned round and hit her in the face with his fist. The blood spirted and made three stains on his shirt.

- 'These stains shall never wash out until I come to remove them myself,' cried the young wife.

- 'And you, unhappy one,' replied the husband, 'you'll not find me again until you've worn out three pairs of iron shoes in seeking me.'

Whilst the blood running from the young mother's nose prevented her from following, the Foal-Man went on his way and was soon out of sight.

Then she had three pairs of iron shoes made, and set out in search of him. She went haphazardly, not knowing which direction to take.

After having walked for ten years, her third pair of iron shoes were almost worn out, when she found herself one day near a castle, where the servants were washing linen by a lake. She stopped for a moment to look at them, and heard one of the washer-women saying:

- 'It's that accursed shirt again! I've tried every way, rubbing it well with soap, and I can't remove the three blood-stains from it; and tomorrow the Lord will need it for going to Church, for it's his best shirt.'

The young woman was all ears. She went up to the washer-woman and said:

- 'Let me have a go at that shirt, just for a moment, please; I think I'll be able to make the stains go away.'

They gave her the shirt; she spat on the stains, soaked them in water, then rubbed them, and they disappeared.

- 'Thanks,' said the laundress; 'go to the castle and ask for

61

lodging; I'll be there shortly and commend you to the chef.'

She went to the castle, ate in the kitchen with the servants, and was told to sleep in a little closet, quite close to her husband's bedchamber. Everyone was in bed. Towards midnight, he went into his bedchamber. The young woman's heart beat so strongly, from finding herself so close to her husband, that she almost fainted. Only a planked partition separated them from each other. She tapped on the partition with her finger; her husband responded from the other side.

She made herself known, and her husband hurried to join her. Just think how happy they were to find one another, after such a long separation, and suffering so many ills!

It was just in time! He was due to marry the Master of the Castle's daughter the very next day; but he put the ceremony off, I don't know under what pretext, and, as the feast had been prepared, and all the guests had arrived, they sat down to eat. The stranger, beautiful like a Princess, despite her dress, was presented to everyone by the *fiancé* as his cousin.

The meal was a happy occasion. Towards the end, the *fiancé* spoke to his future father-in-law as follows*:

- 'Father-in-law, I'd like your advice on this matter: I've a pretty little box, full of precious things, to which I had lost the key. I had a new key made, and now it happens that I've found the first one. Which one should I give preference to?'

- 'You should always respect what is old,' replied the old man, 'you should go back to your old key.'

- 'Well then, here's my first wife, whom I've just found again, for I'm already married; as I still love her, I think I should go back to her, as you said yourself.'

Great was everyone's astonishment; in the middle of the general silence, he took his first wife by the hand, and left the feasting hall with her.

They went back to their land and lived happily together for the rest of their days.

(Told by Barbe Tassel, village of Plouaret, 1869).

---

*Normally it is the heroine of the story who puts forward this dilemma.

Chapter 7. The Toad-Man.

Once there was a good man who had been left a widower with three daughters. One day, one of his daughters said to him:

- 'Would you go and fetch a pitcher of water from the spring, father? There's not a drop left in the house, and I need some for our stew-pot.'

- 'With pleasure, daughter,' replied the old man.

And he took a pitcher and went to the spring. As he was leaning over the water filling his pitcher, a toad jumped up and stuck itself fast on his face, so fast that all his efforts to loosen it were in vain.

- 'You won't get me off, until you promise to give me one of your daughters in marriage,' said the toad.

He left his pitcher by the spring, and ran back to the house.

- 'God! What's happened to you, father?' exclaimed his daughters on seeing the state he was in.

- 'Alas, poor children! This animal jumped on my face just as I was getting water at the spring, and now he says he'll only let go if one of you consents to marry him.'

- 'Good God! What are you saying, father?' replied the eldest daughter; 'marry a toad! It's horrible to look at!'

And she turned away and went out of the house. The second daughter did likewise.

- 'Ah well, poor father,' said the youngest, 'I'll have him as my husband, for in my heart I can't bear seeing you stay in that state.'

Straight away the toad fell on the ground. The wedding was fixed for the next day.

When the bride went into Church accompanied by her toad, the Vicar was quite taken aback, and said he would never marry a Christian to a toad. However he ended up uniting them, when the bride's father had told him the whole story, and promised him lots of money.

Then the toad took his wife to his castle - for he had a fine castle. When it was time for bed, he took her to her room, and there he took off his toad-skin and revealed himself as a handsome young Prince. Whilst the sun was above the horizon, he was a toad; by night he was a Prince.

The young bride's two sisters came to visit her from time to time, and they were quite surprised to find her so happy, laughing and singing all the time.

- 'There's something behind this,' they said to each other; 'we

63

should keep an eye on her and find out.'

They came quietly one night, looked through the keyhole, and were amazed to see a handsome young Prince, instead of a toad.

- 'Hallo! What a handsome Prince!.... If only we had known!'.... they said to each other.

They heard the Prince saying these words to his wife:

- 'I must go on a journey tomorrow, and I'll be leaving my toad-skin in the house. See that no harm comes to it, for I have to use it for another year and a day.'

- 'That's good!' said the two sisters to each other.

Next morning, the Prince left, and his two sisters-in-law came to visit his wife.

- 'God! What beautiful things you have! You must be very happy with your toad!' they said to her.

- 'Yes, sisters, I'm truly happy with him.'

- 'Where's he gone?'

- 'On a journey.'

- 'If you like, little sister, I'll comb your hair for you - it's so beautiful.'

- 'I'd like that very much, good sister.'

She fell asleep whilst they were combing her hair with a golden comb, and then her sisters stole her keys from her pocket, took the toad-skin from the cupboard in which it was locked, and threw it in the fire.

When she woke up, the young woman was surprised to find herself alone. Her husband arrived a moment later, red with anger.

- 'Ah, unhappy woman!' he cried; 'you've done what I clearly told you not to; you've burnt my toad-skin, to my and your mis-fortune. Now I must go, and you shall never see me again.'

The poor woman started crying, and said:

- 'I'll follow you wherever you go.'

- 'No, don't follow me; stay here.'

And he ran off, and she ran after him.

- 'Stay there, I tell you.'

- 'I won't stay, I'll follow you.'

And he kept on running; but run as he may, she kept on his heels. Then he threw a golden ball behind him. His wife picked it up, put it in her pocket, and went on running.

- 'Go back home! Go back home!' he cried again.

- 'I'll never go back without you.'

He threw a second golden ball. She picked it up like the first, and put it in her pocket; then a third ball; but seeing she was still on his heels, he went into a rage and hit her straight in the face with his fist. Blood spirted and three drops fell on his shirt, leaving three stains.

Then the poor woman was left behind, and soon lost sight of the fugitive; but she cried out to him:

- 'Those three blood-stains will never wash out until I find you and make them go away myself.'

Despite all, she continued her pursuit. She went into a great wood. Soon after, whilst following a footpath beneath the trees, she saw two enormous lions sitting on their behinds, one each side of the path. She was quite afraid.

- 'Alas!' she said to herself; 'I think I'm going to lose my life here, for these two lions will surely eat me; but no matter; God keep me.'

And she went forwards. When she came close to the lions, she was quite surprised to see them lie down at her feet and lick her hands. She even stroked them over their heads and down their backs. Then she continued on her way.

Further on, she saw a hare sitting on its behind, by the side of the path, and when she was passing close by, the hare said to her:

- 'Climb on my back, and I'll take you out of the woods.'

She sat on the hare's back, and he soon took her out of the woods.

- 'Now,' said the hare before leaving, 'you're close to the castle where the one you're seeking is to be found.'

- 'Thanks, kind creature of the Good Lord,' said the young woman.

She soon found herself in a great avenue of old oaks, and not far away she saw some washer-women washing linen in a lake. She approached them and heard one of them saying:

- 'Ah! There must be a curse on this shirt; for two years I've tried every way I know to remove the three blood-stains from it, and, although I've tried hard, I can't manage to do it.'

On hearing these words, the traveller went up to the woman who spoke thus, and said:

- 'Please let me have a go at that shirt, just for a moment; I think I'll be able to remove the three blood-stains.'

They gave her the shirt, she spat on the three stains, soaked them in water, rubbed them a little, and they soon disappeared.

- 'A thousand thanks,' said the laundress; 'our Master's about to get married, and he'll be pleased to see the three stains have gone, for it's his best shirt.'

- 'Is there any chance of a job in your Master's house?'

- 'The shepherdess left a few days ago and she hasn't been replaced yet; come with me and I'll recommend you.'

She was taken on as shepherdess. Every day she took her flock
to a great wood which surrounded the castle, and she often saw
her husband walking there with the young Princess who was
going to be his wife. Her heart beat faster when she saw him;
but she did not dare speak.

She still had her three golden balls, and often, to relieve her
boredom, she played bowls with them. One day the young Princess noticed her golden balls, and said to her waiting-maid:

- 'Look! Look! What beautiful golden balls that girl has! Go
and ask her to sell me one.'

The maid went up to the shepherdess and said:

- 'Those beautiful golden balls you have, shepherdess. Would you
sell one to my Mistress, the Princess?'

- 'I won't sell my balls; in my loneliness I've no other pastime.'

- 'Bah! You're unreasonable; look what a state your clothing is
in; sell one of your balls to my Mistress and she'll pay you well;
you'll be able to dress properly.'

- 'I ask neither gold nor silver.'

- 'What do you want then?'

- 'To sleep with your Master for a night!'

- 'What! Wicked girl! How dare you speak like that?'

- 'I will not give up one of my golden balls for any other thing
in the world.'

The maid went back to her Mistress.

- 'Well! What did the shepherdess say?'

- 'I daren't tell you what she said.'

- 'Tell me, at once.'

- 'She said, wicked girl, that she would only give up one of her
balls to sleep for a night with your husband.'

- 'I see! But no matter, I must have one of her balls at any
price; I'll put a drug in my husband's wine at supper time, and
he'll know nothing. Go and tell her that I accept her terms, and
bring me a golden ball.'

That night, on getting up from the table, the Lord was
so sleepy that they had to put him straight to bed. Soon after,
they let the shepherdess into his room. But though she tried
hard, calling him by the tenderest names, embracing him, and
shaking him vigorously, nothing could wake him up.

- 'Alas,' cried the poor woman in tears, 'have I lost after all my troubles; after so much suffering? And yet, I wed you when you were a toad and no one wanted you. And for two long years, in heat and cruel cold, wind, snow and rain, I've sought you everywhere without giving up; and now that I've found you, you sleep like a log! Ah, unhappy me!'

And she sobbed and wept; but, alas, he did not hear her.

Next morning she went into the woods again, with her sheep, thoughtful and sad. The Princess came in the afternoon, as on the previous day, to walk with her maid. On seeing her coming, the shepherdess started playing with the two balls she had left. The Princess wanted to have a second ball, to make a pair, and she said to her maid:

- 'Go and buy me a second golden ball from the shepherdess.'

The maid obeyed, and, to cut the story short, the deal was made at the same price as the day before; to spend a second night with the Master of the Castle.

Once again the Princess put a drug in the Master's wine, so that he had to go to bed straight after supper, and slept like a log. Some time later, the shepherdess was let into his room again, and once more she started to sigh and sob. A manservant who was passing the door by chance, heard a noise and stopped to listen. He was quite astonished by what he heard, and, next morning, he went up to his Master and said:

- 'Master, things happen in this castle that you don't know about, but which you should know.'

- 'Such as?.... Tell me quickly.'

- 'A poor woman, seeming quite unhappy and upset, came to the castle a few days ago, and from feeling sorry for her, they took her on as a replacement for the shepherdess who had just left. One day, when the Princess was walking with her maid in the woods, she saw her playing bowls with golden balls. Straight away she wanted these balls, and sent her maid to buy them at any price from the shepherdess. The shepherdess asked not for gold nor for silver, but to spend one night in bed with you for each one of the balls. She's already given two balls, and spent two nights with you in your room, without your knowing anything about it. It's pitiful to hear her sighing and sobbing. I believe her mind may be deranged, for she says very strange things, such as that she was your wife when you were a toad, and that she's been walking for two whole years in search of you.'

- 'Can all this be true?'

- 'Yes, Master, it's all true; and if you still know nothing

about it, it's because the Princess put a drug in your wine at supper time, so that you had to be put to bed as soon as you got up from the table, and went into a deep sleep till morning.'
- 'Well! I'll have to watch out; you'll soon see some changes here.'

The poor shepherdess was disliked by the other castle servants who knew she spent her nights in the Master's bed, and they only gave her a piece of barley bread, like they gave to the dogs.

Next morning, she went to the woods again with her sheep, and the Princess bought her third golden ball at the same price.

When it was time for the evening meal, the Master kept a careful watch. Whilst he was chatting with the person next to him, he saw the Princess pour a drug in his glass. He pretended not to notice, but instead of drinking the wine, he threw it under the table, when the Princess was not looking.

On leaving the table, he pretended to be sleepy and went to his room. The shepherdess went there also, shortly afterwards. This time he was not asleep; as soon as he saw her he threw himself into her arms, and they wept with joy and happiness at finding each other.

- 'Now go back to your room, poor girl,' he said after some time, 'and tomorrow you'll see some changes here.'

Next day there was a great feast in the castle, for arranging the wedding-day. There were only Kings, Queens, Princes, Princesses and other distinguished persons. Towards the end of the meal, the future husband got up and said:

- 'Father-in-law, I need your advice on this matter: I have a pretty little box with a pretty little golden key; I lost the key and had another one made. But soon after, I found the old key, so now I have two. Which one do you think I should use?'

- 'Always respect age,' replied the future father-in-law.

Then the Prince went into a nearby closet, and came straight back holding the shepherdess by the hand. She was dressed simply, but correctly, and, presenting her to the guests, he said:

- 'Well here's my first key, that's to say my first wife, whom I've found again; I've always loved her, and I'll never have anyone else*.'

And they went back to their country where they lived happily together until the end of their days.... And that's the story of the Toad-Man. How do you like it?

(Told by Barbara Tassel, village of Plouaret, 1869).

*As I have already pointed out, it is normally the Princess who puts forward this dilemma.

The Psyche Myth.

Commentary.

Luzel entitled this section 'The Psyche Myth,' with some trepidation. The title is acceptable provided that no direct borrowing from the Graeco-Roman Tradition is implied. This part could equally have been entitled 'Beauty and the Beast.'

Luzel translated a number of versions of this story, from which we have selected two. All these stories begin with three sisters, two of whom are spoilt and selfish, and a third who is a selfless, Cinderella-like character. In some versions, as in **The Foal-Man**, the first two sisters marry with selfish intentions, and lose; the third sister marries without selfish intent, perhaps because she sees the inner spiritual beauty of her husband, masked by his unpleasant outward appearance. In two other versions of the story, the 'Prince' appears in the guise of a grey wolf and threatens the father with death unless he can marry one of his daughters. In these versions, as in **The Toad-Man**, the daughter is moved to agree to the marriage by compassion for her father. In yet another, probably more recent version, the 'Prince' has his behind stuck in a large cooking pot! In some versions the 'Prince' loses his animal form and reveals his true self as the wedding ceremony takes place; in other versions the 'Prince' is such only at night, and a specific period of time, together with conditions imposed on his wife, is required before he can keep his princely form by day, as well as at night. The wife fails to observe the prescribed conditions, and loses her husband; she has to undertake a long and arduous journey to find him again. There seems to be a gap in the story of **The Toad-Man**, for the wife is only briefly lost in the woods before finding her husband; yet she is later described as having sought him for two whole years! Perhaps Luzel's storyteller had forgotten to include the episode of her having to wear out three pairs of iron shoes before she would find him again.

From an esoteric point of view, these stories are of a spiritual way in which love and devotion, transcending corporeal forms, plays a major role, compared with the importance of action in the earlier stories in this book. There still remains a 'quest' element - symbolised by the heroine's long journey in search of her husband. From a profound point of view, the 'Prince' may be regarded as a God in search of a soul; the heroine representing a human soul seeking God.

PART 5. THE MAGICIAN AND HIS GROOM.

Chapter 8. Koadalan.

Once there was a poor couple who had a son of about fifteen or sixteen. Seeing they were poor and only keeping themselves with great difficulty, they said to their son one day:
- 'You must go away and earn your living somewhere.'
- 'All right,' replied the boy, 'I'll go.'
He was called Yves Koadalan.

His father gave him eighteen small coins, his mother, half a dozen pancakes, and the boy set out.

As he was going along the road, he met a well-dressed noble, who said to him:
- 'Where are you going like that, young man?'
- 'I'm travelling to find work.'
- 'Would you like to come with me?'
- 'Yes; I don't mind who I go with.'
- 'Can you read?'
- 'A little, but not much.'
- 'If you can read, you're not the one I'm looking for.'
And the noble went on his way.
- 'Hello,' said Koadalan to himself, 'I shouldn't have said I could read; I would have been all right with that noble. I'll turn my jacket inside out and get in front of him; he won't recognise me.'

He turned his jacket inside out, ran across the fields, and found himself on the road in front of the noble.
- 'Where are you going like that?' said the latter to him again.
- 'I'm going to look for work.'
- 'Would you like to come with me?'
- 'Willingly.'
- 'Can you read?'
- 'Not at all; my father was too poor to send me to school.'
Then the noble grabbed him and rose up high in the air with him. They alighted near a beautiful castle, in a great avenue of trees, where Koadalan was surprised to see written on the leaves of the trees:- *He who enters here will never leave.* This made him feel like getting away; but how? They went into the castle together, ate together, and, after supper, Koadalan slept well in a feather bed.

Next morning the noble said:
- 'Now I must go away on a journey. You'll stay here for a year and a day. You'll lack nothing in this house. Here's a serviette and, when you want to eat or drink, you'll only have to

70

say to it: "Serviette do your task, bring me this or that," and straight away what you've asked for will appear. Now follow me so I can show you your daily tasks.'

First he led him to the kitchen, where there was a big cooking pot over the fire. - 'Here's a pot under which you must burn two bundles of wood a day, and no matter what you hear, don't take any notice and keep the fire going all the time. Let's go to the stable now. Here's a thin mare with a spiny faggot in front of her, by way of clover; but we give her yet another treat; here's a holly stick with which you'll beat her until you sweat. Take the stick, and let's see if you know how to give a beating.'

And Koadalan beat the poor beast with all his might.

- 'Good, good! You're not bad at it. Now this young foal you see here must be given as much clover and oats as it wants. Now we'll go inside. Here's a door you must never open, nor this one. Note them well, for if you come to open one of these doors, you'll regret it! As for the rest of the castle, you may go as you please and open any doors you wish.'

After having given all his instructions, the noble went away.

- 'Now then, where am I here?' said Koadalan to himself; 'with the devil, perhaps? But let's see first if what he said about the serviette is true. - Serviette, do your task! Bring me some bacon and roast meat, and some good cider and wine!' And straight away it all appeared on the table. - 'A marvel,' he said to himself, 'it's all going well.' And he got drunk and slept at the table. As soon as he woke up, he said to himself, 'it's high time I set to work.'

And he went and made a hellish fire under the big cooking pot; and he heard a strange noise, like the sighing and moaning of souls in pain; but he didn't worry much about it, and went to the stable. He gave clover and oats to the young foal, then he took his jacket off, picked up the holly stick and set to beating Teresa as hard as he could. (That was the mare's name).

- 'Stop, wicked boy, have mercy on me,' cried the mare.
- 'What! You speak as well, do you?'
- 'Yes, for I wasn't always a mare like this, alas!'
- 'Then where can I be, where the animals speak like people?'
- 'You're at the castle of the greatest magician on earth, and if you don't watch out, the same will happen to you as happened to me, and perhaps even worse.'
- 'And can no one get away from here?'
- 'It's difficult; and yet, if you do what I tell you, perhaps we'll

both be able to escape from the grips of this demon.'
- 'Tell me quickly, for I'm ready to do anything to get away from here.'
- 'Go to the two rooms you have been forbidden to enter, and you'll find two red books in one of the rooms, and one in the other. Bring these three books, and, as you can read, you yourself will become the greatest magician in the world, and by losing them, the master of this castle will also lose all his power.'

Koadalan went to the two forbidden rooms and took the three red books.
- 'Good,' said Teresa; 'now read them.'

Koadalan started reading, and, as he read, he saw horrible, frightening things; but he also learnt all kinds of secrets, above all, ways of changing his form and likeness at will.
- 'Now,' said Teresa, 'there's an eagle on top of the highest tower, and if it sees us leaving it will make such an uproar with its wings and cry out so loud that the magician will hear it, no matter where he is, and he'll come running at once. You must tie it up with its wings and head between its feet. It's sleeping just now.'

Koadalan went to find some rope, and tied up the eagle's wings and head, then he went back to Teresa.
- 'Now you must set fire to the great pile of wood in the court-yard.'

Koadalan set the pile of wood alight, and there was a hellish fire.
- 'There still remains a bell which rings itself when anything unusual happens in the castle; you must take its tongue out (its clapper), and then stuff it with oakum.'

Koadalan took the bell's tongue away, and stuffed it.
- 'Now, to become a handsome Prince, go and wash your head in the water of the spring at the bottom of the courtyard.'

He washed his head in the spring, and straight away his hair became golden.
- 'Now wrap straw and oakum round my feet, so I won't make any noise on the courtyard pavement as we leave.'

He did that as well.
- 'Now take the sponge, the bundle of straw, the curry-comb, and above all, don't forget your three red books. - That's it. - Now climb on my back, and let's go quickly.'

The eagle could no longer cry, nor the bell ring, and they left at a triple gallop (literally, a red gallop).

After some time, Teresa said to Koadalan:
- 'Look behind; can you see anything coming?'
- 'Yes, a pack of dogs; and they're running, and how!'
- 'Quick, throw the bundle of straw behind you.'
He threw the bundle of straw, and the dogs leapt on it and ran back to the castle with it.
- 'Look behind again,' said Teresa a moment later; 'can you see anything?'
- 'There's only a cloud coming towards us, and it's so black that it's blotting out the daylight.'
- 'The magician's in the middle of that cloud. Quick, throw the curry-comb behind you.'
He threw the curry-comb; the magician came down from the cloud, picked it up, and took it back to the castle.
- 'Look behind again,' said Teresa a little later, 'can you see anything?'
- 'Yes, there's a flock of crows flying towards us.'
- 'Quick, throw the sponge!'
He threw the sponge; and the crows took it back to the castle.
By now, poor Teresa was tired out; but she was full of courage.
- 'It's only another seven leagues to the river,' she said, 'and if we can cross it, we'll be saved, for then the magician will have no more power over us; but look behind you again, can you see anything?'
- 'Yes, my God! There's a black, bearded dog on our heels!'
Just as Teresa jumped in the river, the dog bit at her tail and tore out a mouthful of horsehair. But he was just too late!
- 'You're lucky to have escaped from my land,' he said, showing his teeth.
- 'Yes,' replied Koadalan; 'I can laugh at you now, and I've got your three red books.'
- 'Yes, unfortunately; but those books will come back home to me.'
- 'We'll see about that.'
And the magician left in fury, making fire and thunder.
Koadalan and Teresa continued on their way, but quite at ease now, and free from all cares. They came to a great rock in a wood, where Teresa said:
- 'Now you must kill me.'
- 'God! What are you saying? I could never do that.'
- 'You must kill me, I tell you, or everything we've done up till now will be lost. Cut my throat, open up my belly, and then see what happens.'

Koadalan killed Teresa, opened up her belly, and was surprised to see a most beautiful Princess emerge.

- 'I am the daughter of the King of Naples,' she said; 'but I am not destined for you; another, more beautiful than I, will be your wife, the King of Spain's daughter. But should you need help at anytime whatsoever, come here and say three times: "Teresa! Teresa! Teresa!" And I'll come at once.'

They said their goodbyes with tears in their eyes. But let us leave the Princess now, and follow Koadalan.

- 'What I'd best do now,' he said to himself, 'is to go towards Spain, for that's where the one who will be my wife is to be found. But which road should I take?'

He dressed himself as a Prince (with the three red books he had kept, he could do anything he wanted), and he soon found himself in Spain. He presented himself at the King's palace, and asked to speak with him. The King gave him a good reception, because he took him for his nephew, the son of the King of France, whose looks and manners had been taken by Koadalan.

Two or three days after his arrival, he was walking with the King in his garden, and asked him:

- 'I thought you had a daughter, uncle?'
- 'No, nephew, I've no daughter.'

He had one, but he did not wish it to be known, and he kept her shut in a tower with a waiting-maid. He went to see her once a day; but he always went there alone.

Next day, when Koadalan was walking again with his uncle in the garden, he was surprised to see a golden ball rolling along the path and coming to a stop against his foot.

- 'What's this golden ball?' he said.
- 'It's nothing,' replied the King.

It was from his daughter, who was playing bowls with her maid on the flat roof of her tower and who had thrown this ball deliberately in the garden when she had seen the handsome Prince walking with her father. Koadalan had also noticed the Princess. - 'Sooner or later,' he said to himself, 'I'll find a way of speaking to her.'

He got up at midnight, and, thanks to his books, he came to her bedroom door without anyone seeing or hearing him. He tapped on the door: Tap! Tap!.....

- 'We don't open this door to anyone. Who are you?'
- 'The son of the King of France.'
- 'My cousin! Then we'll open it for you.'

And the Princess opened the door, and they embraced like

74

cousins, and he stayed in her room with her until daybreak. And from then on, he came back every night, without anyone knowing anything about it. But soon the Princess felt she was going to be a mother. The King continued to visit her every day, and, noticing she was becoming plump, he said one day:

- 'Your food is doing you good, daughter.'
- 'Yes, surely, father; and then I've no cares.'

When the time came, she gave birth to a son, a fine child. When the King came, as usual, and saw the child in it's cradle, and his daughter ill in bed, he went into a terrible rage, and left cursing. Despite all, he told his nephew nothing of this. But seeing he had become sad and worried, the latter said to him one day:

- 'Uncle, why are you so sad and worried these days?'
- 'Alas, I've a daughter whom I've kept from everyone's eyes; she sees only me and her waiting-maid, and yet she's given birth to a son.'
- 'Yes uncle, I know about it; I'm the child's father, and I ask you to give me his mother's hand.'
- 'Well! Since it's happened, what can I do better than to give her to you; I'd rather you marry her than another.'

And they were married straight away. But the old King no longer showed any signs of joy. He died soon after, and Koadalan succeeded him on the throne. The latter had little taste for his new way of life, and, after a year, he wanted to go back to his country. As he still had his three red books, he asked for a fine carriage, and straight away one came down from the sky. All three of them climbed in it, father, mother, and son, and the carriage went up high in the air like an eagle. By chance it passed by the front of the castle of the great magician Foulkes. The latter lived in a golden castle held between heaven and earth by four gold, and four silver chains. Foulkes was at one of the windows, and, on seeing Koadalan pass by, he begged him to come down and pay him a short visit. Foulkes had also tried to have the King of Spain's daughter, but he had not succeeded. He had recognised her as soon as he saw her passing by. Koadalan, who mistrusted no one, stopped with pleasure at Foulkes' castle, and the latter made him welcome. After supper, he led him and his wife to a beautiful bedroom, and their child was entrusted to a wet-nurse. Unfortunately, before getting in bed, Koadalan forgot to put his three red books under the pillow, and when he woke up next morning, Foulkes had stolen them. Poor man; he was lost! Foulkes threw him down a very deep well (it was more than a league deep) and he landed in the middle of a great forest.

- 'My God, where am I now?' he asked himself; 'what can I do now that I've lost my three red books? And what's worse, is that my wife and son are in the power of that accursed traitor Foulkes. This time, I'm done for. If only I could find the wood where I said goodbye to Teresa; but where is it?'

He went around the forest, and met neither man nor beast. Night came, and he slept with his head on a large mossy stone. At daybreak he looked around and recognised the rock near the place where he had said goodbye to Teresa.

- 'Hello,' he said, 'there's still a chance.'

And he shouted three times: 'Teresa! Teresa! Teresa!' and straight away Teresa came and said:

- 'Do you need me, Koadalan?'
- 'Yes, surely Princess, for I'm in great difficulty.'
- 'I know all about it: You've lost your books, and your wife and son; but if you do exactly what I tell you, you'll get them back again.'

Then she took him before Foulkes' castle, and said to him:

- 'Everyone's asleep now in the castle. Go very quietly to Foulkes; you'll find him asleep in bed, and on a little table near-by, you'll see the three red books. Take them, come back quickly, and during that time I'll find your wife and son.'

Koadalan went to the bedroom where Foulkes was stretched out in bed snoring; he took the three red books, and fled quickly. Teresa was waiting with his wife and son. They embraced and wept with joy.

- 'Before leaving,' said Teresa, 'what do you want me to do with Foulkes?'
- 'Now that I've got my three books back, and my wife and son, I no longer wish him ill.'
- 'Then let's go, and quickly.'

When they were in the middle of the forest, Teresa said again:
- 'Now I'll say farewell to you for always, for we shall never meet again.'

And she rose up in the air, and was soon out of sight.

Koadalan, his wife, and his son climbed back into their carriage which came as soon as he asked for it, and they quickly reached Plouaret in Koadalan's country. They were all quite astonished on seeing such a handsome Prince and so beautiful a Princess. No one recognised Koadalan, not even his father and mother, who were old by then, and still very poor. They had a magnificent castle built. But the aged parents stayed in their thatched cottage; they preferred it that way, and their son never left them short of anything and gave them all the money they wished.

One day Koadalan said to his father:

- 'Tomorrow, father, there's a good fair at Lannion, and you should go there.'

- 'Why go to the fair, when I've neither horse, cow, nor pig?'

- 'Don't worry in the least about that; tomorrow morning you'll find a superb steer in your outbuilding. Take it to the fair and ask whatever price you wish for it; even if it were a thousand, you would get it. But don't give the rope with the steer. Take great care about that, otherwise you'll never see me again.'

- 'All right,' said the good man.

Next morning old Koadalan went to his outbuilding, and was quite surprised to find a magnificent steer, the finest he had ever seen. He put a rope round its neck, and went to Lannion with it. Everyone who saw him on the way, said: 'What a fine steer! Whose is it?' And the old man was quite proud.

As soon as he reached the fair-ground, the crowd pressed in around him.

- 'How much for the steer?' asked the butchers of Lannion and Tréguier.

- 'A thousand,' said the old man. And they went away.

It was the same with the dealers from Morlaix and Léon. None of them took the steer away.

Then there came three unknown dealers, their pockets stuffed with money (they were three devils):

- 'How much for the steer?' they said.

- 'A thousand!'

- 'You're not selling it for nothing, grandfather. Anyway it's a fine beast; we like it and we're agreed. Here's payment in cash.'

The old man put the money in his pocket and handed the steer over to the three dealers; but he kept the rope.

- 'Give us the rope as well, grandfather.'

- 'I've only sold the animal, and I won't give the rope.'

- 'The rope always goes with a cow or a steer.'

- 'I didn't sell the rope and I'll not give it under any circumstances.'

- 'We need a rope, however; give us that one and we'll give you another thousand.'

- 'I won't give it, not even for ten thousand!'

And the old man put the rope in his pocket, and left.

Then the three dealers climbed on their steer. But straight away the latter began to bellow, and ran like it was crazy, throwing the three dealers on the ground. Right away the steer changed into a dog and ran off home. The three dealers ran after it, in the form of three wolves. But the dog reached Koadalan's door first, and went in by a single leap. Straight away it became a man, for it was Koadalan himself. The three wolves, changed into three dealers, stopped at the door.

- 'A little too late, boys,' said Koadalan from his home.
- 'We almost got you; but it doesn't matter, we'll get you by the scruff of the neck yet.'
- 'We'll see about that.'

And they left in raging anger.

When father Koadalan came back home:
- 'Well, father, did you do well at the fair?'
- 'Yes indeed; a thousand! And I've brought the rope back; here it is.'

Some time later, Koadalan said to his father:
- 'There's a fair at Morlaix tomorrow, father; it's a good fair and you should go there.'
- 'And with what?'
- 'With a horse that you'll find in your stable tomorrow; the best horse you've ever seen. You can ask two thousand for it, and you'll get it. But don't give the bridle; take great care not to do that.'

Next morning, father Koadalan found a magnificent horse in his stable, just like his son had said, and he took it to Morlaix. Everyone admired the horse. 'How much? How much?' asked the dealers; but when they heard 'two thousand' they all went away.

Soon the three dealers from Lannion* arrived again:
- 'How much for the horse, grandfather?'
- 'Two thousand.'
- 'Agreed! It's ours!' And they shook hands on it.
- 'Let's go to the inn, to count the money and have a drink.' They went to the nearest inn. The old man had one too many and got drunk, so drunk that he forgot to keep the bridle.

The three dealers took the horse with its bridle on its head. All three of them climbed up on it. Everyone looked at them with astonishment.

*(Luzel's storyteller is mistaken here; the three dealers were unknown, and not from Lannion.)

- 'Where do these three imbeciles come from?' they said. They went along the Quay of Léon, and the urchins yelled out and even threw stones at them.

- 'You three idiots,' said an old man to them, 'you've less sense than your animal; at least two of you should get down; aren't you ashamed?'

All three of them got off. Then the horse jumped in the river and changed into an eel. The three dealers dived in, changing into three big fish to pursue the eel. But the latter then flew off in the form of a dove, and flew high up above the town. The three big fish followed it again, in the form of three sparrow hawks. The dove, tired out by its flight and seeing that it was about to be caught, saw, as it passed above a castle, a maid busy filling a bucket at a spring. It fell into the bucket in the form of a golden ring. Straight away the maid took the ring, slipped it on her finger, and ran to the castle. Then the three sparrow hawks changed into three musicians, and went, each with a violin, to play music under all the castle windows. Lords and ladies came to their windows to listen and throw money to them.

- 'Thank you,' said the musicians, 'but it's not money we're after.'

- 'Then what do you want?'

- 'A golden ring that the maidservant found when she was getting water at the spring.'

- 'You shall have it.'

They went to look for the maid. The latter was in her room, busy admiring her ring. She was terrified on suddenly seeing a handsome Prince next to her, and the ring disappear from her finger.

- 'Don't be afraid,' said the Prince to her, 'I'm the golden ring that was on your finger. Your Master is coming to ask for this ring (for I'm about to change back to a golden ring on your finger). But don't give it him until he promises to do what I'm about to tell you. Tell him to set fire to the great pile of wood in the courtyard; then, when the fire's at its hottest, throw the golden ring in it, and tell the three musicians to go and get it.'

As soon as he had spoken these words, he changed back into a golden ring on the maid's finger. Right then the Master came and said to the maid:

- 'Where's the golden ring you found when you were getting water at the spring?'

- 'Here it is, my Lord.'

- 'Give it to me.'
- 'My Lord, I've been strongly advised not to do so until you agree to what I'm about to ask: Set fire to the great pile of wood in the courtyard; when the fire's at its hottest, I'll throw the golden ring in it, and say to the musicians: Go and fetch it.'

They set light to the pile of wood, then the maid threw the ring in the middle of it, and said to the musicians: 'Go and fetch it.'

Straight away the latter threw themselves in the flames and started looking for the golden ring, like real devils, which is what they were.

But the golden ring had changed itself into a charred grain in the great pile of wheat in the castle granary. Straight away the three others became three cocks which set to seeking the grain in the wheat-pile. But the charred grain became a fox which gobbled up the three cocks!

And that's how Koadalan won his victory over the three devils, and how he kept his three red books.

After so many trials, Koadalan returned home. His father was dead; his wife and son died soon afterwards, and he found himself alone. But he still had his three red books. With them he could do whatever he wished; everything, except avoid death. And he was already old, and he feared death very much! Every day he studied his books more and more, seeking the secret of immortality. One day he thought he had found it, and this is how: He called all his household, and said to them:

- 'Obey me completely, no matter what I tell you to do, and I'll give you as much gold and silver as you wish. First of all go and find a woman breast-feeding her first-born child and bring her and her child here.'

They brought such a mother with plenty of milk. She had to stay in the castle for six months, without seeing any man, not even her own husband. Koadalan said to her: - 'Now I'm going to be put to death and chopped up like sausage meat; then the chopped-up bits of my body will be placed in a big earthenware pot. This pot will be buried in a heap of hot manure, and, for six months you must come and sprinkle your milk over the manure above the pot, twice a day, at midday and three o'clock, for half an hour each time. But take great care you don't fall asleep whilst you're sprinkling the milk. If you do exactly as I've said, after six months I'll come out of the pot in one piece, full of life and in good health, stronger and handsomer than ever before; then I'll never die again. - Tell me if you'll do it. You'll be paid a hundred a month.'

- 'Yes,' she said, 'I'll do it.'

Then he called his servants and said to them:

- 'Now you must put me to death, and chop all my body into little pieces like sausage meat. Then you must put all the bits, and the blood, in a big earthenware pot which you must cover over with a cloth and then bury it in a heap of hot manure, where it must stay for six whole months. After six months, you'll see me come out full of life, healthy, and stronger and handsomer than ever. Have no fear, for it will all happen just as I've told you. Will you obey me?'

- 'Yes,' replied the servants.

They did everything as he had said. They put him to death, chopped him in little bits as fine as sausage meat, then they put all of him, including the blood, in a large pot which they buried in a heap of hot manure.

Twice a day, half an hour at a time, the wet-nurse went and sprinkled her milk over the manure above the pot. She had done it for five months.... five-and-a-half months; there was only three days to go till the end of the six months, when she fell asleep whilst sprinkling her milk on the manure heap.

Then Koadalan died, alas!

When they dug into the heap they found his body entire, coming up through the manure and about to stand up. Three days more, and he would have succeeded! But he was dead, alas, quite dead from having tried to make himself immortal!

(Told by Jean-Marie Guezennec, carpenter, Plouaret, 1869).

The Magician and his Groom.

Commentary.

Luzel gives several stories under the heading of 'The Magician and his Groom.' The story of Koadalan seems to be the most complete, so much so that Markale entitled it 'The Saga of Koadalan.' Another version, Ewen Congar, has, however, a more authentic beginning. In Ewen Congar, a bright young boy asks his father, a poor widower, to send him to school. The father says he cannot afford it, but the boy persuades him to sell his two cows, and then his horse, to keep him at school for three years. The teachers are pleased with the boy's progress and he leaves school with a great deal of knowledge for his age. Before setting out on his journey, he has a reversible outfit made, black one side, white on the other. Unlike the introduction to Koadalan, that to the story of Ewen Congar seems more authentic by stressing the young man's intelligence, and explaining why he would not be recognised when he turned his jacket inside out. The rest of the story of Ewen Congar is, however, incomplete compared with that of Koadalan.

Koehler, commenting on this story in the 1870's saw it as composed of heterogeneous elements, and having a link with the story of the 'Sorcerer's Apprentice.'

Markale, writing more recently, was struck by the links between this story and parts of the Mabinogion.

In the first part of the story, Koadalan meets Teresa, the Mare-Goddess, and a foal which is given abundant food. Markale regards Teresa and the foal as equivalent to Rhiannon and her son Pryderi held prisoner in a castle in the story of Manawyddin in the Mabinogion. He points out that Luzel made it clear that his storytellers often altered names of people and places to those familiar to their listeners. Koadalan means Wood-Alan (or Coed-Alun, in Welsh). Teresa initiates Koadalan into the mysteries of the castle, and helps him to escape. The fact that Koadalan is destined not to marry Teresa, but another Princess, may be evidence that the former is to be understood as a Goddess. Teresa helps him again, in the second part of the story. Markale implies that Koadalan should be understood as confused with Prydri, first introduced as a foal.

The three red books taken from the castle have something of the quality of talismans, for their possession is important, as well as that of the knowledge derived from them. From these books Koadalan acquires the shamano-druidic science of metamorphosis, a mastery over the animal kingdom.

The Magician and his Groom.

The three demons who came in search of Koadalan and his red books, should more correctly be regarded as three magicians.

In the third part of the story, Koadalan uses his science of metamorphosis to escape from his pursuers, and, finally, to rid himself of them. Markale regards this part of the story as the Armorican version of the legend of Keredwen and Taliesin, regarding Keredwen as an appearance of the 'Great Queen,' or Mother-Goddess of ancient times.

The story of Koadalan starts off as a story of the spiritual quest: A young man sets out on a journey, and is helped through the dangerous psychic domain by a Goddess. In achieving the first part of the quest he acquires magical knowledge, which becomes a distraction, preventing him from travelling further along the spiritual path. At the end of the story he tries to achieve physical immortality, albeit through his own death and renascence. Even in this unsuccessful operation he is not, however, a wicked magician, and he does not seek immortality through harming others, but only through his own death.

PART 6. THE THREE BROTHERS.

Chapter 9. Princess Marcassa.

Once there was a King of France, who had three sons.

The two eldest were handsome, strong and vigorous. The youngest, on the contrary, was puny and sickly. He rarely left the corner by the fire, and for this reason they had nicknamed him Luduenn, meaning Little Cinders.

The old King was ill. All the doctors of the land had visited him, but they had been unable to do anything for his illness.

A magician who had also been called, said the King could only be cured by touching the Dredaine-Bird* in its golden cage.

- 'Where can this bird be found?' asked the King.

- 'In Princess Marcassa's castle; it's beyond the Red Sea, and it's surrounded by three high walls, with three courtyards defended by giants, seven-feet tall, and dragons which spit fire for seven leagues all around.'

- 'And who's going to fetch me the bird from this castle?' asked the King, with a smile.

- 'I'll go, father,' said the eldest son.

And he took as much gold and silver as he wanted, mounted the best horse from the palace stables, and left saying: 'If I'm not back in a year and a day, it will be because I'm no longer alive.'

Well, he rode and he rode, so much and so well that he reached the land of the Saxons**. He asked for the castle where the Dredaine-Bird could be found, and they smiled and laughed at him.

He went to an inn where he found pretty girls and pleasant companions, and stayed there as long as his money lasted.

The year and a day went by, and, seeing that he had not come back, the second son went to his father and said:

- 'A year and a day has gone by, and my brother hasn't come back. I wish to go and look for him, and also for the Dredaine-Bird which, alone, can bring about your recovery.'

And he set out, taking a lot of gold and silver with him. He reached the same inn as his elder brother, and stayed with him, leading the same life-style.

The year and a day went by, and, seing he had not returned, Luduenn went to his father, whose condition grew worse each

---

*The bird's name must have been altered, but I cannot see what it might have been originally.

**Bro-Saoz, land of the Saxons, is the Breton name for England.

day, and told him he also wished to go in search of his two
elder brothers and the Dredaine-Bird.
- 'You as well, son?' replied the old man; 'stay at home
to close my eyes, for you'll never succeed in this enterprise,
seeing that your two brothers haven't done so.'
   Luduenn persisted in his requests to go. His father gave him a
little money, much less than he had given the others. He went
to the palace stables, took a dromedary which could do seven
leagues an hour, and set forth.
   He reached the town where his two brothers had stopped, and
asked for the castle where the Dredaine-Bird could be found.
They told him that no one had ever heard tell of it, except for
two foreign Princes, who had been in the town for some time,
where they were living it up. He asked to see them. They took
him to the inn, and he recognised his two brothers and was
happy to see they were still alive. They took his money from
him, and then sent him away.
   Poor Luduenn went on his way, sad at heart because of
the way his two brothers had treated him.
   Thanks to his dromedary, he covered a lot of ground in a
short time.
   Night came upon him when he was in a great forest. It was
dark and he could hear wild beasts crying out from all sides. He
climbed a tree and saw a little light in the distance. He climbed
down, went in the direction of the light, and reached a poor
hut made of tree branches, thatched with hay. He met a little
old woman there, and asked her for a night's lodging.
- 'I can't put you up, son,' she replied; 'I haven't a bed for you.'
- 'I'll sleep on the hearthstone, grandmother.'
- 'All right, come in then, for I feel sorry for you.'
   Luduenn tied his dromedary to a post, and went inside.
- 'It smells bad in here,' he said, putting his hand over his nose.
- 'Yes, it's my poor husband; he's been dead for eight days and
his body's still here.'
- 'Why don't you bury him?'
- 'Alas, my boy, I've no money, and our parson won't do some-
thing for nothing.'
- 'How much does he want?'
- 'A six-franc piece, and I haven't a farthing.'
- 'I'm not rich, but tomorrow morning I'll have your husband
buried, grandmother.'
   Next morning he went to see the parson and said:
- 'Here's the money you asked for, to bury the poor woman's

husband from the forest; bury him straight away.'

The corpse was buried, and Luduenn and the old woman were the only mourners.

Luduenn went on his way straight after the funeral. Whilst he was crossing a great arid plain, he noticed he was being followed fairly closely by a white fox.

- 'Why is this animal following me?' he asked himself.

At the end of the plain, to his great astonishment, the fox spoke to him:

- 'You're looking for the Dredaine-Bird?'
- 'Yes, truly, God's good creature; can you tell me something?'
- 'Yes, you're not far off; can you see the castle up there, on the mountain? That's where it is, and this is what you must do to take it away with you. To enter the castle you must cross three courtyards, each surrounded by high walls. The first is full of snakes, toads, and other venomous reptiles; in the second, there are snakes and tigers, and in the third, snakes and giants, who defend the castle entrance. All of them sleep deeply, from eleven o'clock until the last chime of midday, stretched out all over the floor, with their tongues hanging out. You may go amongst them and even step on them without fear of waking them up, before the last chime of midday. Once in the castle, you'll find, without any difficulty, three beautiful rooms, and in a fourth (I say nothing of what you'll see in the first three), you'll see the Dredaine-Bird in its golden cage, hanging from the ceiling by three golden chains. It will also be asleep. Nearby, a sword will be hanging from a golden nail in the wall. Take the sword, cut through the three chains, and take the bird away in its cage. But don't forget to do all of this before the last chime of midday, if not the doors will close on you, and you'll never come back.'

Luduenn thanked the fox for its advice, armed himself with courage and went on his way.

He reached the castle just as eleven o'clock was chiming, and found the door to the first courtyard open. He went over the threshold and saw the floor littered with enormous snakes and other hideous reptiles; in the second and third courtyards, his heart almost stopped at the sight of the monsters surrounding him and exhaling a nauseating and suffocating smell. At last, despite all, he went into the castle. He crossed a first room without seeing any living being. But he found a crust of white bread on a table, and, as he was hungry, he cut off a good slice and ate it. He was surprised to see that the crust did not diminish when it was cut; he put it in his pocket, saying to himself: 'This could be useful when I'm travelling.' He went into the second room, and saw a jar of wine on a table, with a glass beside it: 'A marvel!' he said to himself; and he drank a glass, then two, then three, without the wine in the jug diminishing. He put it with the bread in his pocket, and went into the third room. There he went into ecstasy, his mouth open at the sight of a Princess, beautiful as the day, and lying on a purple bed in a deep sleep. The wine had gone to his head and made him bold, and he took his shoes off and kissed the sleeping Princess.

He did not forget what the fox had said, however, and went into the fourth room.

There he saw the Dredaine-Bird asleep in its golden cage hanging from the ceiling by three* golden chains. He saw the sword hanging from the wall, and on its blade he read the words: 'He who possesses me can kill ten thousand men, striking with the fine edge, and cut whatever he pleases, using the opposite edge.' - 'That's good,' he said; and he took the sword, cut the three golden chains with three good blows: Swish! Swish! Swish!... And he ran off with the bird in its cage, without forgetting the sword. He ran over the bodies of the snakes and giants, who were still sleeping with their tongues hanging out, and, just as he was crossing the threshold of the outer courtyard, the first chime of midday struck. - 'It's all going well so far,' he said to himself. And he mounted his dromedary, which was waiting at the door, and left at hurricane speed.

When the Princess, the giants, snakes and other reptiles woke up, on the last chime of midday, they knew straight away that the bird had been stolen; the snakes started belching flames, and the giants set out in pursuit of the thief. Luduenn's and his dromedary's hair was burnt. But the dromedary kept up a good pace, guided by the white fox which ran ahead of it, and they reached the limits of the domain of the Magician of the Golden Castle, beyond which he had no more power. They were saved. Then the white fox disappeared, and Luduenn went peacefully on his way.

At the end of the great desolate and arid plain he had just crossed, he found a good roadside inn, and he went inside to eat a little, and take a rest. He asked for the best things in the inn. The bread was not to his liking; he asked for the head waiter, and said to him:

*The storyteller was uncertain if there were three, or four golden chains.

- 'Your bread's no good at all.'
- 'There's no better in the land,' he replied, 'and it's the one eaten by the King himself.'

Luduenn pulled the crust from the Golden Castle out of his pocket, saying: 'I've got better.' He cut a slice and gave it to the head waiter.

- 'Taste this, and tell me what you think of it.'

He tasted it and found it so delicious that he asked for more. Luduenn cut him another slice and let him see that his crust did not diminish. - 'If you had bread like that,' he said, 'you would soon make a fortune.'

- 'That's true; where can I get some?' he asked.
- 'Oh, nowhere; it's unique.'
- 'If you would sell it me, I would pay you well.'
- 'How much would you give me?'
- 'A hundred.'
- 'Give me the hundred and it's yours, on condition however that you'll give it back to its owner, the Princess of the Golden Castle, if she ever comes to claim it back.'

He accepted, thinking it unlikely that the Princess would ever come from the Golden Castle to claim it back.

Luduenn continued on his way. Towards sunset he stopped at a second roadside inn, and sold the jar of inexhaustible wine to the innkeeper for two hundred. Then he rode and he rode until at last he reached the land of the Saxons. He went to look for his brothers in the inn where he had left them. They gave him bad news. After having foolishly spent all their money, they had become thieves. They had been caught and put in prison, prior to being put to death.

The King, however, was engaged in a terrible war with the Emperor of Russia; he was having a hard time and had forgotten about his two prisoners.

Luduenn resolved to go and offer his services to the King.

The doorman tried to stop him from going into the palace; but he showed him his sword and went in. He managed to reach the King and showed him his sword, explaining its power and promising to help him against his enemies if he would set his brothers free.

The King accepted, and the two Princes were set free. Then Luduenn marched against the Russians at the head of the army, and, thanks to his sword, the sight of which was enough to rout the best soldiers, he won a total victory.

Seeing that his brothers had debts everywhere, and especially

at their inn, Luduenn sold his sword to the innkeeper on condition that he would settle the debts and give the sword back to
the Princess of the Golden Castle, if she ever came to claim it
back.

Then the three brothers left with the Dredaine-Bird in its
golden cage. Luduenn always carried the cage and never put it
down. His two elder brothers were jealous of his success and
plotted to get rid of him, in order to have the bird and give it
to their father as their own conquest. When they were passing
a deep well by the roadside, they leant over the opening and
exclaimed:

- 'What a pretty flower there; come and look at it, Luduenn,
you've never seen anything like it.'

Luduenn put his cage on the ground and ran and leant over the
opening of the well. His two brothers grabbed his feet and threw
him down the well, then they left, taking the bird in its golden
cage, and the dromedary.

When they reached home, the old King was very low. He
improved a little on hearing the news of the arrival of the
marvellous bird, which should return him to health, and there
were, on that occasion, festivals and banquets.

However the bird was very sad, and when they took it into the
King's bedchamber, it became angry, making a terrible noise and
not letting anyone touch it. The old monarch weakened every
day, and those close to him became most concerned.

But let us now go back to Luduenn and see what happened to
him in his well.

Fortunately the water was not deep. The white fox soon came
to his aid. It dropped its tail into the well, and it lengthened
until it reached the water, then it told Luduenn to hold on, and
it pulled him out of the well. Then it spoke to him as follows:

- 'You should continue on your way back home, which you'll
be able to do now without difficulty. A little way from here,
you'll meet an old beggar and you should give him all the money
you've got. You should also change clothes with him, and present
yourself like that at your father's, where you should ask for any
work whatsoever, the most humble possible. Don't worry about
the rest, it will all go well, and the baddies will get what they
deserve. Do you remember having stayed a night in a hut where
a poor woman's dead husband was rotting because she hadn't the
money to bury him, and you paid the burial expenses?'

- 'Yes, I remember it clearly.'

- 'Well, I'm the soul of that poor man for whom you paid the last rites. Now I'll say *adieu*, for you'll never see me again in this world.'

And then the fox disappeared.

Luduenn continued on his way and soon met the old beggar he had been told about. He gave him all his money, and changed clothes with him. He walked and he walked, without becoming discouraged, and ended up at his father's palace. His eldest brother, who was in the courtyard when he went in, said: - 'Send him to look after the pigs' - which they did. Soon after, they made him a stable-boy, and, as he looked after his horses well, they became fat and shiny and full of zest. The King was very pleased with his work and often spoke of him. Then his brothers, who had recognised him, started to look for a way of getting rid of him. They advised their father to give him the task of feeding the Dredaine-Bird. The bird was so bad-tempered since its arrival at the palace, that it bit everyone who approached it, but when it saw Luduenn it began to sing and flap its wings as a sign of joy. Luduenn took it on his finger and went into the King's bedchamber with it. The King felt better as soon as he heard it sing; but to be fully cured, he needed to lie with Princess Marcassa.

The Princess had had a son, a superb child, nine months after Luduenn's visit to the Golden Castle. One day, the child asked its mother who was its father, and she replied that she did not know.

- 'I want to go and find my father,' replied the child, 'and I won't stop till I've found him.'

And he set out, accompanied by his mother.

They stopped for refreshment at the inn where Luduenn had left the bread which did not diminish when it was cut. They were served this bread, and the Princess realised that Luduenn had passed that way.

- 'Give me the bread,' she said to the innkeeper.

- 'I won't give it to anyone in the world,' he replied, 'unless it's to the Princess from the Golden Castle, should she ask for it back, one day.'

- 'I'm the Princess of the Golden Castle and the bread belongs to me and I'm taking it.'

And she put it in her pocket. For the rest, the innkeeper had already made his fortune with it.

The Princess and her son went on their way, and came to the second inn Luduenn had stopped at. They stopped there also, found the jar of inexhaustible wine, and took it with them.

Then they came to the land of the Saxons and went to the inn where Luduenn had left his enchanted sword. They took it also.

- 'Don't despair,' said the Princess to her son, 'we're getting closer to your father.'

They continued on their way and reached Paris.

The Princess had herself announced at the King's palace. The old monarch was full of joy on hearing this news, and, although ill, he went down to the courtyard and offered his hand to help her down from her gilded carriage.

- 'I'll not get down from my carriage,' she said, 'until he who took the Dredaine-Bird from my castle comes to offer me his hand.'

- 'I'm the one,' said the eldest son, coming forward.

- 'Tell me, then, how my castle is guarded.'

And since he could say nothing except that the castle was surrounded by high walls, the Princess said to him:

- 'It's not you; go away.'

- 'I'm the one,' said the second eldest, coming forward.

- 'How is my castle guarded?' the Princess asked him.

And since he replied no better than the first:

- 'It's not you either; clear off!'

'If they don't bring me the man who took the Dredaine-Bird from my castle, I shall go away.'

Then Luduenn went towards her, dressed as a stable-groom, and said:

- 'I'm the one, Princess.'

- 'Tell me how my castle is guarded.'

- 'Your castle, Princess, is surrounded by three high walls with three courtyards. In the first courtyard, there are snakes and all kinds of venomous reptiles; in the second there are more snakes, and lions and tigers; and in the third, snakes and enormous giants, and they belch flames for seven leagues around.'

- 'You know something, you,' said the Princess, 'but tell me more.' - 'All these beasts and monsters,' replied Luduenn, 'sleep deeply, stretched out on the courtyard pavings, from eleven o'clock to midday, and I profited from this to pass by them unharmed. In the castle's first room I found a piece of bread which did not diminish when cut; I ate some of it and I took it away; in the second room, there a jar of wine which was inexhaustible; I drank well from it and I also took it; in the third room, I saw a Princess, beautiful as the day, who was in a deep sleep on a purple and gold bed.'

- 'And what did you do then?' asked the Princess.

The Three Brothers.

- 'I contemplated her for some time with my mouth wide open, but, as the wine had gone to my head a little, I was bold and lay on the bed alongside her, and gave her a kiss.'
- 'That's it,' said the Princess, 'and here's your son' - and she showed him her son - 'but go on.'
- 'Then I went into a fourth room where the Dredaine-Bird was sleeping in its golden cage hanging from the ceiling by three golden chains. I saw a sword hanging from a golden nail on the wall; a sword which I took and used to cut the golden chains holding the cage. Then I fled as quickly as possible, carrying the bird, sword, wine-jar and bread.'
- 'And where are they?' asked the Princess.
- 'The bird's here; as for the bread, wine-jar, and sword, I left them in the inns where I stopped for the night.'
- 'I've found them and brought them with me,' said the Princess;'but the bird - you must let me see it.'

Luduenn went to fetch the bird in its golden cage.

When it saw the Princess it flapped its wings as a sign of joy, and sang so loud and harmoniously that its song echoed repeatedly throughout the palace and all who heard it rejoiced - except for the two elder brothers.

The Princess took it out of its cage, put it on her finger and presented it to the King, telling him to stroke it with his hand.

The bird, so unmanageable until then, let the old King touch it and stroke it, and straight away he found himself completely cured and rejuvenated.

Then the Princess told them all of the way Luduenn had been victimised by his two elder brothers, and asked that the latter should be treated as they deserved.

The old monarch was furious, and cried out:
- 'Heat up an oven and throw them in.'
Which they did.

Then Luduenn married Princess Marcassa, and there were, on that occasion, great festivities and banquets, where the old King forgot to watch himself, and died, they say, of indigestion.

Then Luduenn was crowned King in his place*.

(Told by Marie Manac'h, maidservant, Plougasnou, 1875).

*This story, which could also come under the heading of 'The Golden-Haired Princess,' has striking similarities to a Slav story published by M. Alexandre Chodzko, entitled 'Obnivak or the Fire-Bird,' in his book 'Contes des Paysans et des patres Slaves.'

The Three Brothers.

Commentary.

In **Princess Marcassa** the story begins with three brothers, each obliged to set out on a quest for their father's sake. The two elder brothers set out with worldly intentions of honour and bravado, seeking a reward of earthly fame, rather than from any real concern for the King, their father. They soon become discouraged, and worldly temptations distract them from their quest. The third brother, Luduenn, sets out with a selfless intent, and, advised by the fox in return for a virtuous deed, he succeeds in traversing the dangerous 'other world' - the psychic domain - returning home with a 'treasure.'

We have already seen other situations where an adventure is initiated by the father's plight, as, for example, in the 'Toad-Man.' The crust of bread which never diminished, and the jug of inexhaustible wine may be compared with the serviette in the story of Koadalan. They may be understood literally, or, from a more profound point of view, as representing inexhaustible means of spiritual sustenance. Markale regards such things as representing the grail, particularly the pre-Christian grail. The incident where Luduenn is cast into a well by his brothers, reminiscent of Joseph in the Bible, occurs in other Breton tales. The old King dies as soon as Luduenn marries the Princess; just as in the story of Koadalan. In some other Celtic stories, for example that of Kulwch and Olwen, Yspaddaden, the King, has to be killed before the marriage can take place.

Luzel gave eight stories under the heading of the 'Three Brothers.' Perhaps the best-known of them is the story of three brothers who share their inheritance of a cat, a cock, and a ladder. The brother who inherits the cat makes his fortune as did Dick Whittington. Massignon, who gave a version of this story in which the cock was replaced by a scythe, traced the earliest printed version back to 1535. Despite its age as a printed work, this story seems to have lost whatever mythological character it may have had, and Luzel only included it in his book with hesitation. We have selected the story of Princess Marcassa as being more ancient and 'authentic' in character.

We have already seen a number of stories in which several brothers, or sisters, are involved, and in which one, often the one considered most unlikely, succeeds. In all these stories, it is not the physical appearance of the brothers or sisters which is important (despite the 'ugly sisters' of pantomime). The real difference is between the worldly, and the selfless, character.

PART 7. WICKED STEPMOTHERS AND WITCHES.

Chapter 10. The Cat and the Two Witches.

Once there was a fair young girl who had a stepmother who never wished her any good. She was called Annaic. Her father loved her, but his wife did all she could to make him detest her. One day she went to see her sister, who was a witch, and asked her how she could get rid of Annaic.

- 'Tell her father,' replied the witch, 'that she's leading a life of shame, and he'll send her away.'

But the father did not wish to believe all the bad things they said about his daughter, and the stepmother went back to consult her sister again.

- 'Well then,' said the latter, 'here's a cake baked in my style for you to give to the young girl; as soon as she's eaten it, her belly will swell like a pregnant woman's, and then her father will be forced to believe what you tell him about her bad behaviour.'

The wicked stepmother went back home with the bewitched cake, and gave it to Annaic, saying:

- 'Here you are, child, eat this honey-cake; I've made it myself, specially for you.'

Annaic took the cake and ate it, without suspicion and with pleasure, believing that her stepmother was at last showing her a sign of affection. But soon after, her belly swelled up so that all who saw her thought she was pregnant, and the poor girl was full of shame and did not know what to think.

- 'Didn't I warn you,' said the triumphant stepmother to her father, 'that your daughter's been behaving badly; look what a state she's in.'

Then the father put Annaic in a barrel and pushed it out to sea. The barrel broke up on some rocks. Annaic climbed out unharmed, and found herself on a desert isle which seemed uninhabited. She went into an underground grotto, dug out of the cliff, and was surprised to find a little bedroom, fully furnished with a bed, some earthenware vases, and a fire burning in the hearth. She thought it must be inhabited; but after waiting a long time without anyone coming, she lay on the bed and slept peacefully.

Next morning, on waking up, she found herself alone. She got up and went to the rocks to collect shellfish for her breakfast; then, for the rest of the day, she went all over the island without finding any habitation nor meeting any human being. In the evening she went back into her grotto and slept there again,

94

peacefully; and she did likewise throughout the following days.

When her time came, she gave birth to a..... little cat. Great was her sadness when she saw what she had brought into the world; but she resigned herself to it, saying:

- 'It's the will of God.'

And she brought up her little cat as though it were a child.

One day when she was weeping and moaning her lot, she was most surprised to hear the cat speak, in human voice, as follows:

- 'Console yourself, mother, I'll look after you; it's my turn now, and I won't let you go short of anything.'

And the cat took a sack, which was lying in a corner of the grotto, put it over his shoulder, and went out. He ran all over the island, found a castle, and went in. The inhabitants of the castle were astonished to see a cat walking upright on its hind legs and carrying a sack over its shoulder, like a man. He asked for bread, meat, and wine, and they did not dare refuse him, so strange did it all seem to them. They filled his sack and he went away. He returned to the castle every other day, and each time, he went back with his sack full, so that his mother was never short of anything in her grotto.

One day, the son of the castle had been involved in a lawsuit; having lost the papers which could have obtained him a pardon, he was sent to prison. Everyone in the castle was upset, and when the cat came as usual, he asked why they seemed so sad. They told him; then they filled his sack, as usual, and he went back. When he reached the grotto, he said to his mother:

- 'Sadness and desolation reign in the castle.'

- 'What's happened?'

- 'The young Lord was involved in litigation; he lost his papers and they've put him in prison; but I'll go and find him tomorrow, in his prison, and I'll tell him that, if he'll marry my mother, I'll find his papers and give them to him.'

- 'How can you ever think he'll take me for his bride, child?'

- 'Perhaps he will, mother; let me try.'

Next day the cat went to the prison and asked to speak to the young Lord. But the jailer tried to drive him away with his broom. The cat jumped up on his face and clawed at his eye, then, he climbed up the wall and went through the window into the prison, and said to the prisoner:

- 'My good Lord, you've been feeding my mother and I since we've been on this island, and, in return, I'll get your papers back and get you out of prison, if you'll promise to marry my mother.'

- 'What, poor animal, can you speak as well?' asked the young Lord, astonished.

- 'Yes, I can also speak, and I'm not what you think; but tell me, will you marry my mother?'

- 'Marry a cat, me, a Christian? Who do you think I am?'

- 'Marry my mother, and I tell you, you won't regret it. I'll give you until tomorrow to think about it; then I'll come back.'

And he went away.

He came back next day with the young Lord's papers, and said to him:

- 'Here are your papers; promise me you'll marry my mother, and I'll give them to you, and what's more, I'll have you set free here and now.'

The prisoner promised, and he was set free.

The cat's mother had a Godmother who was a witch, who knew of the situation they were in. She came to see her when the cat was away, and spoke as follows:

- 'The young Lord's got his papers back, and he's promised to marry you. When the cat comes in, take a knife and cut his belly open, without any hesitation, for straight away he'll become a handsome Prince, and you yourself will become a beautiful Princess. Then you'll be able to go and marry the young Lord, and I'll send you fifty fine horsemen for your wedding-day procession.'

When the cat came in, his mother opened up his belly. Straight away a handsome Prince, magnificently dressed, came out of the skin, and she herself became a beautiful Princess. The fifty horsemen also arrived, and a fine gilded carriage came down from the sky. The Prince and Princess climbed in it, and set off to the castle accompanied by the fifty horsemen.

The young Lord, who was at his window, was surprised to see such a fine group of strangers arriving. He hurried down to greet them. The Prince came towards him holding the Princess by the hand, and introduced her, saying:

- 'Here's my mother; you promised to marry her - how do you like her?'

The young Lord was so overwhelmed by what he saw and heard that he lost command of his speech, and could only babble:

- 'God! What a beautiful Princess!.... Yes, certainly!.... How?.... It's too great an honour!....'

The wedding took place there and then. During the wedding feast, which was superb, they heard music such as is only heard

The Cat and the Two Witches.

in Paradise, without seeing anything. It was the bride's God-
mother, the witch, who had sent her invisible musicians. She also
gave her a beautiful gilded carriage, and said:

- 'You've only to say " gee up " and my enchanted horses will
lift you up in the air and take you wherever you wish. But, if
you go home to your father, take care you don't let your stepmother embrace you; as for your father, I'll say nothing; you
can embrace him as often as you wish.'

Then they climbed in the carriage which lifted them above the
clouds and took them straight to her father's home. The latter
recognised his daughter at once, and showed great joy at seeing
her again, embracing her tenderly. The stepmother was furious;
however she hid her anger, wicked woman, and tried to embrace
her as well; but the Prince cried out to her:

- 'What are you up to, you? You won't embrace my mother;
instead you'll be paid back as you deserve.'

And they set fire to a great pile of wood and burnt the stepmother, her daughter, and the witch as well.

Then, for eight whole days, there were all kinds of festivities,
with music, dancing, and banqueting.

(Told by Marguerite Philippe, Plouaret, 1869).

Chapter 11. The Night-Dancers.

Listen if you wish,
Here's a pretty little story,
In which there's never a lie,
Except, perhaps, for a word or two.

Once there was a rich widow who married a rich widower.

The man had a pretty, well-behaved daughter by his previous wife, called Lévénès; the widow also had a daughter by her first husband, called Margot, who was bad and ugly.

The husband's daughter, as so often happens in such cases, was detested by her stepmother. They lived in a fine manor house, at Guernaour, near Coathuel. At the crossroads at Croaz-ann-neud, which is on the road going from Guernaour to the village of Plouaret, the night-dancers were often seen in those days, or so they say, and whoever passed them as they danced in circles in the moonlight and did not wish to dance with them, became a victim of their bad humour.

The Lady of Guernaour knew this well, and, one Sunday evening, after supper, she said to Lévénès:

- 'Go and fetch my book of hours, which I've left in Church, beneath my pew.'

- 'Yes mother,' replied the young girl.

And she went alone, although night had already fallen.

It was a clear moonlit night. When she reached the crossroads, she saw a crowd of little men who were dancing in a circle, holding hands. She was afraid, poor child, and thought of going back, but her stepmother would grumble and perhaps beat her, so she resolved to pass them. One of the dancers ran after her and asked her:

- 'Would you like to dance with us, pretty girl?'

- 'Willingly,' she replied, trembling.

And she joined in the circle and danced.

Then one of the dancers said to the others:

- 'What present should we give this charming girl, for dancing with us?'

- 'She's quite pretty, but she should become even prettier,' said one of the dancers.

- 'And at each word she speaks, a pearl should fall from her mouth,' said a second.

- 'And everything she touches with her hand should change to gold, if she wishes it to,' said a third.

- 'Yes, yes,' cried all the others together.
- 'Many thanks, sirs, I'm much obliged,' she said with a curtsy.
Then she went on her way.

When she reached the village, she went to the sacristan's, for the Church was locked, and she told him why she had come.

The sacristan went with her and unlocked the door. She touched the door with her hand, and it became gold, and, with every word she spoke, a pearl fell from her mouth. The sacristan could not believe his eyes and was dumbfounded. He picked up the pearls and put them in his pocket. Lévénès went inside, took her stepmother's book from her pew, and went straight back home.

The night-dancers were no longer at the crossroads when she passed by.

- 'Here's your book of hours, mother,' she said, giving her a golden book.
- 'What,' she asked her, surprised to see her back unharmed, 'you didn't see the night-dancers?'
- 'Yes I did,' she replied, 'I saw them at the crossroads.'
- 'And they didn't hurt you?'
- 'No, quite the opposite; they're very pleasant, these little men; they invited me to dance with them.'
- 'And did you?'
- 'Yes, I did.'
- 'That's good; go to bed.'

The stepmother had noticed her stepdaughter's extraordinary beauty, and also the pearls which fell from her mouth, each time she spoke, and the way her book of hours had changed into gold; but she had pretended not to notice, but inside herself she thought:

- 'Good! I know what to do; tomorrow night I'll send my own daughter to the night-dancers; these little men have inexhaustible treasures of gold and pearls hidden underground and amongst the rocks.'

Next day, at the same time, she said to her daughter Margot:

- 'Margot, you must go and fetch me another book of hours from my pew in the Church.'
- 'No, I won't go,' replied Margot.
- 'I want you to, and you're going,' replied the mother, 'and when you pass by the crossroads, if you see the night-dancers and they invite you to dance with them, do so, and have no fear; they'll do you no harm, but quite the contrary, they'll give you a fine present.'

Margot answered rudely, and her mother had to threaten her with a stick, to make her go.

When she reached the crossroads, the night-dancers were dancing in circles in the moonlight. One of them ran up to Margot and politely invited her to dance with them.

- 'Shit,' she replied.
- 'What present should we give this girl, for the way she has welcomed our proposition?' said the dwarf to his companions.
- 'She's quite ugly, but she should become uglier yet,' replied one of them.
- 'She should have only one eye, in the middle of her head,' said another.
- 'A toad should fall out of her mouth with each word she speaks, and everything she touches should be dirtied by it,' said a third.
- 'That's what should happen,' cried all the others in a chorus.

Then Margot went to Church, took her mother's book from her pew, and went back home.

- 'Here's your book,' she said, throwing it at her, all dirty and smelly.

And at the same time, three toads fell from her mouth.

- 'What's happened to you, poor child?' cried the mother, upset; 'what a mess you've come back in!.... Who did it to you? Did you see the night-dancers, and did you dance with them?'
- 'Me?... Dance with such ugly creatures! Shit on them!'

And again she spat out as many toads as words she had spoken.

- 'Go to bed, daughter,' said her mother, furious at what she saw, and promising herself revenge on Levénès.

But fortunately, the latter was married shortly afterwards, to a young gentleman of the land, who took her to his castle, and the stepmother and her daughter almost died of spite and jealousy.

The young wife soon became pregnant. Her father was dead. She gave birth to a son, and chose her stepmother as his God-mother, for she had neither hatred nor resentment over the ill-treatment and humiliation she had received from her. The evil stepmother went to a witch she knew, and asked her how she could substitute her own daughter in place of the young mother, without her husband knowing it. The witch said:

- 'Pass a black needle through the mother's head, and straight away she'll be changed into a wild duck and fly out of her bed-room window, to go amongst the ducks on the lake. Then you

100

can put your daughter in the bed, close the bedroom windows and tell the husband she's ill and can't bear the light.'

She did as advised, and it all happened as planned.

The young mother was changed into a duck, on the lake, whilst Margot was in bed, taking her place.

When the husband came to his wife's bedside, to ask how she was, he found all the shutters closed.

- 'How are you, little darling?' he asked her.

- 'Shit!' replied a rude voice, with unbearably smelly breath.

- 'Alas!' he cried, 'my poor wife's really ill, she's delirious. Open the windows, mother-in-law, so I can see her, for it's too dark in here.'

- 'The light upsets her,' said the midwife, won over by the step-mother.

The husband was upset; he didn't want to leave her bedside by day nor by night; he slept in the same room, but they gave him a soporific, and he slept like a log.

Whilst everyone in the castle was asleep, except for the wet-nurse, who was watching over the child in its cradle, the mother came in through the window, which they had opened for a change of air. She was in the form of a wild duck, and began to fly around the cradle, saying:

- 'I'm sorry for your lot, poor child! I'll come and see you twice more like this, but if they don't remove the black needle from my head by the end of the third night, I'll stay a duck until I die. And your father, alas, asleep next to the one in my place, neither knows I'm here nor hears me.'

Then she went out through the window and back to the lake.

The wet-nurse, who had heard and seen everything, said nothing to anyone, although she found it strange.

When the husband woke up in the morning, he asked the one he believed was his wife, how she was; but again she replied rudely, and his sadness only increased.

- 'No doubt it's the effect of a milk fever,' the wet-nurse said to him, 'and it will soon go.'

Before going to bed, the husband again drank a soporific, without knowing it, and slept as deeply as the night before.

When they were all asleep, the duck came again and said:

- 'Alas, poor child, your father's asleep again and can't hear me! I'll come again tomorrow night, for the last time, and if no one pulls the black needle out of my head, I'll have to leave you and your father for always.'

And she went away again, after having flown around the cradle for a long time.

The wet-nurse heard it all again, and told herself:

- 'Whatever happens, I must warn the Master of what's going on here; I can't bear seeing that duck suffer so; there's something behind all this.'

Next day, when the father came to see his child, she said:

- 'I've something on my mind that I must tell you. You don't know what goes on here, at night.'

- 'What then, nurse? Tell me, I beg you.'

- 'They make you drink a soporific just before you go to bed, and you know nothing of what's going on around you; they're deceiving you, and the one you think is your wife is Margot, your wife's stepsister. Your wife's been changed by witchcraft into a duck, and now she's on the lake with the others; but at night, when everyone's asleep, she comes to see her child. She's already been twice. She'll come tonight for the last time, and if you pull out a black needle they've passed through her head, she'll return to her previous form; if it's not done tonight, she'll stay a duck forever.'

- 'I thought something strange was going on in the castle,' said the husband; 'but tonight I'll be on my guard, and we'll see.'

When bedtime came, the stepmother poured the husband a drink. He pretended to drink it, but threw it under the table when no one was looking.

Towards midnight, the duck came through the window again, and said:

- 'I've come to see you for the last time, poor child, and your father's no doubt asleep again....'

On hearing these words, the latter jumped out of bed, where he was pretending to be asleep, and exclaimed:

- 'No, I'm not asleep this time!'

And he took hold of the duck, pulled out the needle, and straight away she returned to her original form and threw herself on the cradle and embraced her child.

- 'Light the lamp and call the stepmother,' he cried.

The wicked stepmother came; but when she saw how things had turned out, she tried to flee with her daughter.

- 'Not so fast,' cried the young Lord; 'wait a moment, for each should be paid according to his works.'

And he had an oven made white-hot and they threw them in.

As for the others, they lived happily for the rest of their days.

(Collected in Plouaret, 1869)

Commentary.

Luzel gave five stories under this heading. The obvious Cinderella-theme is perhaps too well-known to require much comment. In fact, in one of Luzel's stories, the stepdaughter is given the job of looking after a bullock; when it is killed and opened up, they find a pair of golden slippers inside. As would be expected, they fit her perfectly, but when the stepmother tries to substitute her own daughter on the wedding day, the latter is unable to walk, for they are too tight for her.

In the two stories we have translated, we find a hero and heroine each transformed into animal form, victims of the kind of witchcraft derived from shamanism. This may indicate an ancient, pre-Christian origin for these tales.

The second story, The Night-Dancers, is really two stories joined to make one, for the first part, the meeting with the night-dancers, occurs elsewhere as a story in its own right, independent of the stepmother-witch theme. The best-known independent version is that of the 'Two Hunchbacks and the Dwarfs.' In Luzel's version of the latter story, the first hunchback dances innocently and happily with the dwarfs. Their song is limited to a repetition of the first three days of the week, in French:

Lundi, mardi et mercredi
Lundi, mardi et mercredi
....and the first hunchback adds two more days:
Et jeudi et puis vendredi
....which pleases the dwarfs. As a reward they offer him gold and silver, or to have his hump taken away. He refuses the treasure and goes home no longer a hunchback. The second hunchback, seeing his friend returned to normal physique, goes to dance with the dwarfs. He adds the last two days of the week, in French:

Et samedi et dimanche*
....but this does not rhyme with the rest, and the dwarfs are upset and add the first hunchback's hump to his own.

In another version of the 'Hunchbacks and the Dwarfs' given by Tranois, the second hunchback angers the dwarfs by asking for the treasure the first hunchback had refused. This modification seems more convincing, for in this case the second hunchback is punished for his covetous intention. There remains also the possibility that the dwarfs, not being Christian, are angered by the mention of Sunday.

*Disul, in Breton.

103

PART 7. THE BODY WITHOUT A SOUL.

Chapter 12. The Body Without a Soul.

The first part of Luzel's story is so similar to the first part of the story of Koadalan, that we summarise it as follows:

A French Prince goes hunting and follows a wounded crow under a large stone. The Prince falls down a deep hole into another world, where he takes on the job of looking after a magician's castle for a year and a day. His daily tasks include looking after caged birds, horses (except a little black horse, which he has to ill-treat), and a collection of pistols. He begins his tasks as instructed, but when he beats the little black horse, it speaks to him and warns him that he might end up the same, so he begins to treat it well. Soon after, he notices that one of the birds, a sparrow, has a pin through part of its head; he withdraws it, and it becomes a beautiful Princess, who tells him that the little black horse is her brother. He spends a happy year with the Princess, who is such by day, but returns to her cage as a bird at night. When the magician is due to return, she tells him that he will let him choose a bird, a horse, and a pistol. She advises him to choose the sparrow (herself), the little black horse, and the least attractive of the pistols. She further advises him to fire the pistol at a copper head above the door; this will break the magician's spells, and deliver all those he has enchanted. When all this is accomplished, they leave together in a gilded carriage which takes them to the court of France. The Princess warns him that on his return he must not let any other woman embrace him, or she will straight away be carried off by the Body Without a Soul. As one might expect, a young cousin approaches him from behind and kisses him; a carriage comes down from the sky, and the Body Without a Soul carries the Princess away.

The Prince is inconsolable. He sets out on a quest for the Body Without a Soul. He meets a hermit who has never heard of the Body Without a Soul, but who gives him a serviette-talisman which will provide him with instant food and drink. He continues on his way and, on an immense empty plain, he meets an army of ants, big as hares, which seem about to attack and devour him. He spreads out his serviette and tells it to feed all the ants, which it does. In return, two of them, the King and Queen of the Ants, tell him they will help him if ever he is in need. He continues on his way, and meets a second hermit, who tells him the Body Without a Soul lives in a castle suspended between heaven and earth by four golden chains, and that it is so high up that it cannot be seen from the ground. The hermit adds that he is master of all the winged animals, and that if ever he needs his assistance, he will only have to call him. The hermit advises him to go to the seaside, where he will find a little fish stranded. He goes and finds the fish, and puts it back in the water; as we would expect, it turns out to be the King of the Fish, and offers to help him, if ever he is in need. The story continues:

After walking along the shore for some time, he saw the chains which held the Body Without a Soul's castle. They were sealed in two enormous rocks. He stopped to think, and said to himself:

- 'How can I reach the castle?.... If I had wings, perhaps - but the old hermit said even the eagle couldn't fly that high!... What shall I do? Who can help me?.... Perhaps an ant, climbing the whole length of the chain, link by link, could reach the castle? The King of the Ants promised to help me if I needed it; I'll call him and see:

King of the Ants, I call for your help

To climb to the castle of the Body Without a Soul.'

And the King of the Ants came straight away, and asked:

- 'What can I do for you, son of France?'

- 'I'd like, if it's possible, to be changed into an ant, so I'll be able to crawl up this chain to the castle.'

- 'It shall be as you wish,' replied the King of the Ants.

And the Prince was instantly changed into an ant. Without wasting any time, he started crawling up the chain, link by link; he did it so well that he reached the castle, and what a fine castle it was - he marvelled when he saw it. He crawled over the castle walls and through a window into a room where the Princess was playing cards with the giant. He climbed up her dress, and hid in her sleeve. It was night time and, about midnight, the giant retired to his room, leaving the Princess alone.

- 'I wish to become a man again,' thought the ant; - and the Prince was instantly returned to his original state.

- 'My God! Dear Prince,' exclaimed the Princess; 'how did you manage to get here? Alas, you're lost, poor friend, for no one ever gets away from here alive.'

The Prince told her how he had got there, and pressed her to leave with him, without wasting any time.

- 'And the giant; you've not thought of him?'

- 'I'll kill him!'

- 'You can't do that; his life doesn't reside in his body!'
- 'And where the devil is it, then?'
- 'I don't know; but I'll find out for you, tomorrow.'
- 'How?'
- 'Every night, after supper, he comes here to play cards with me; you can hide yourself as an ant in my sleeve, and, as he suspects nothing, I'll get him to say how his life can be taken.'

They spent the night together, sleeping very little, for they had so many things to talk about. When day broke, the Prince changed into an ant, and spent the whole day hidden in her sleeve. After supper, the giant played cards with the Princess, as usual. Suddenly, the Princess said:

- 'Do you know what a strange dream I had last night?'
- 'What did you dream about? Tell me, I beg you.'
- 'Oh, it was only a foolish dream. I dreamt that a young Prince had come to the castle, and that he wanted to kill you in order to carry me off to the court of France, and marry me. Wasn't it a foolish dream?'
- 'Ah yes, quite stupid, for no such thing can happen; no man can climb up here from earth; and, even if that did happen, I can't be killed like other men; my life doesn't reside in my body.'
- 'Really? Then where is it?'
- 'That's a secret that I've never told anyone, but I can tell you; listen: My life resides in an egg, that egg's inside a dove; the dove's inside a hare; the hare's inside a wolf; and the wolf's locked in an iron trunk at the bottom of the sea. Do you still think it would be easy for someone to take my life?'
- 'Oh no, certainly not.'

The Prince heard everything. As soon as the giant retired to his room, he returned to his natural form, and the Princess asked him:

- 'Well, did you hear everything?'
- 'Yes.'
- 'And do you still think we can get away from here?'
- 'Perhaps yes; you must trust me, and we'll see later. For the moment, I must go back to earth, but when I come back, I'll have the giant within my grasp.'

As soon as day broke, the ant went down the chain, and, as soon as he was by the sea, he called the King of the Fish:

'King of the Fish, come quickly,
For I need your help.'

And a moment later he saw a little fish lift its head out of the water, and say:

106

The Body Without a Soul.

- 'What can I do for you, son of France?'
- 'Somewhere under the sea, there's an iron trunk containing the life of the Body Without a Soul; I'd like to have it.'

The King dived down to his palace and ordered his heralds to call all the fish of the sea, great and small.

The heralds blew into their conch shells, and they came from all sides. The King took a great book containing all their names, and ticked them off as he questioned them about the trunk. Not one of them had seen it. They had all answered the call except for a little fish which they did not think much of. At last, it came, excusing itself for being late. It had been delayed, because it had stopped to examine the trunk! The whale was sent, with the little fish as guide, to fetch the trunk. Three fish, smaller than the whale, took the trunk to the beach, where they left it at the Prince's feet. The latter opened it, for the key was in the lock, and an enormous wolf jumped out. Straight away, the Prince chopped its head off with an axe, then he opened its belly. A hare jumped out, but he grabbed it by the ears and opened its belly also, and the dove slipped through his fingers and flew off: Flap! Flap! Flap! - What should he do? for he had nothing to shoot it with. He thought of the old hermit who was master over the winged animals, and called for his aid. The hermit sent a sparrow-hawk after the dove, which took it and returned it to the Prince's hands. He opened it up and took the egg containing the giant's life. He returned to the castle by the same means as before, with the egg in his pocket. The giant was stretched out in bed, very ill and almost dying. With each animal killed by the Prince, he had visibly weakened, just as if someone had cut one of his limbs off. The Prince went in his room in his natural form; the giant tried to throw himself at him, but his strength failed him; then the Prince threw the egg so it broke on his forehead, and he expired there and then. Straight away the chains holding the castle broke with a frightful din, and everything fell to the bottom of the sea.

The Prince and Princess had already escaped in the giant's carriage, and soon they were in France, at the King's palace. Everyone was delighted to see them, and they were married several days later, and there was, on that occasion, feasting and rejoicing such as has never been seen since in the land.

I myself was there turning the skewers, but as I put my finger in all the sauces, a great devil of a chef kicked me right to Plouaret to tell you this story.

(Told by Catherine Doz, village of Plouaret, 1869).

The Body Without a Soul.

Commentary.

The legend of the *Body Without a Soul* occurs in many parts of the world.

Luzel's version of this story starts off with the part Markale considered to be derived from the same roots as the story of Rhiannon and Pryderi held prisoner in an enchanted castle, in the Mabinogion.

Other Breton versions of this story start with a soldier (a knight?) returning home. He hears of a Princess who has been delivered to, or taken by, a monstrous Body Without a Soul, and he sets out on a quest to rescue her. In these versions, as in the present one, the hero is initiated into shamanism by meetings with animals, and hermit-shamans living in the forest. The hero then uses his shamano-druidic powers to overcome the Body Without a Soul, and deliver the Princess.

Markale points out that in some tribes where shamanism is still practised, it is forbidden to wake a sleeping shaman. The reason given is that during sleep, the shaman's soul leaves his body and travels elsewhere; a sudden awakening could leave the soul wherever it is, and the body without a soul. The latter then becomes a monstrous being.

Markale sees this story as representing a newly-initiated shaman-druid, who possesses his own soul, opposing and supplanting an older shaman-druid who has lost his soul.

This story, in fact, is really two stories in one: The story of the Body Without a Soul, and the story of the Castle in the Air. The latter story also occurs in the Breton Tradition, independent of the body-without-a-soul theme.

The story of the Castle in the Air is of a type we have seen several times already: A hero sets out on an adventure, or quest, to another world, the domain of a magician, and steals a treasure (a Princess) which he brings back with him. Once again the symbolism is of man's quest for the 'spirit hidden within himself,' held prisoner by a powerful monster, whose powers are man's worldly attachments and vices.

REFERENCES.

Bullfinch, Thomas. **The Age of Chivalry and Legends of Charlemagne.** Mentor.
New York. 1962.

Head, Joseph, and Cranston, S. L. **Reincarnation, an East-West Anthology.**
Julian Press. New York. 1961.

Humphreys, Emyr. **The Taliesin Tradition.** London. 1983.

Koehler, Reinhold. Commentary on **Koadalan.** Revue Celtique 1, p. 132 et. seq.
Paris. 1870-1872.

Luzel, F. M. **Koadalan.** Revue Celtique 1, pp. 106-131. Paris 1870-1872.

Luzel, F. M. **Contes Populaires de Basse-Bretagne.** Paris 1879.

Markale, Jean. **La Tradition Celtique en Bretagne armoricaine.** Payot. Paris. 1984.

Massignon, G. **Contes Traditionels des Tailleurs de Lin du Tregor.** Picard. Paris.
1984.

Tranois, Corentin. **Histoire de Coulommer et de Guilchand.** Revue de Bretagne,
tome II. p. 109. 1833.

(**Note** – the stories in this book are taken from Luzel's 'Contes Populaires,' except for the story of 'Koadalan,' which is taken from Revue Celtique, 1).

INDEX.

Note - the above index includes few names of places or people; they are of little importance, for the storytellers have altered the ancient names to ones familiar to their listeners.

Also published by Llanerch:

L. Wieger.

WISDOM OF THE DAOIST MASTERS.

Léon Wieger's classic translation of the works of:
Lao Zi (or Lao tsu)
Lie Zi (or Lieh Tsu)
and
Zhuang Zi (or Chuang Tsu)
....updated in modern Pinyin spelling.

ISBN 0947992022

Published by Llanerch Enterprises, Llanerch,
Felinfach, Lampeter, Dyfed. SA48 8PS.
Printed by Cambrian News, Aberystwyth.